A CAUSE WORTH DEFENDING

NORMAN FINN

Primix Publishing
East Brunswick Office Evolution
1 Tower Center Boulevard, Ste 1510
East Brunswick, NJ 08816
www.primixpublishing.com
Phone: 1-800-538-5788

Published by Primix Publishing: 06/26/2025

ISBN: 979-8-89194-520-3(sc)
ISBN: 979-8-89194-529-6(hc)
ISBN: 979-8-89194-521-0(e)

Library of Congress Control Number: 2025911298

CONTENTS

DEDICATION

To: Ted, Leslie, Taylor, And Rachel Finn

"No man can answer for his courage If he has never been in peril."

—La Rochfould

FORWARD

I spent considerable time researching this book as I did "I Shall know who I am" and "A Cause for All".

Michael Jannsen is once again called upon to use his unique abilities to combat the dangers to his family, his world, and heritage. My aim in writing the manuscript was to blend fact with fiction and create a story that portrays the actual events and the adventure.

I welcomed the challenge and wrote while trying to come to grips with my wife's passing.

In a way the book was therapeutic keeping me occupied and my imagination working overtime. As in my other writings, I had spent time in most of the places Michael visited.

This book is quite different than the others. The history and the political complexities of the events brought out an entirely different set of circumstances that Michael encountered. The actual facts were eye opening to the author and I believe will be to the reader.

The years spent in the fashion business were a key factor in telling a story within a story. In a sense I was reliving a part of my life through Michael's exploits.

I hope my story telling and factual accounts will give you some insight into the world that stood on the brink. Michael's adventures may help understand the significance of those times.

As an afterthought,

I was in Israel on October 7th and experienced firsthand the horrors of war. They say history repeats itself. There are definite similarities between Oct 6,

1973 and Oct 7, 2024.

My thanks to Dr. Ruth Khowais who was instrumental in offering me another viewpoint and edited the manuscript. This book would not have happened without the sources listed and the Internet.

Norman Finn

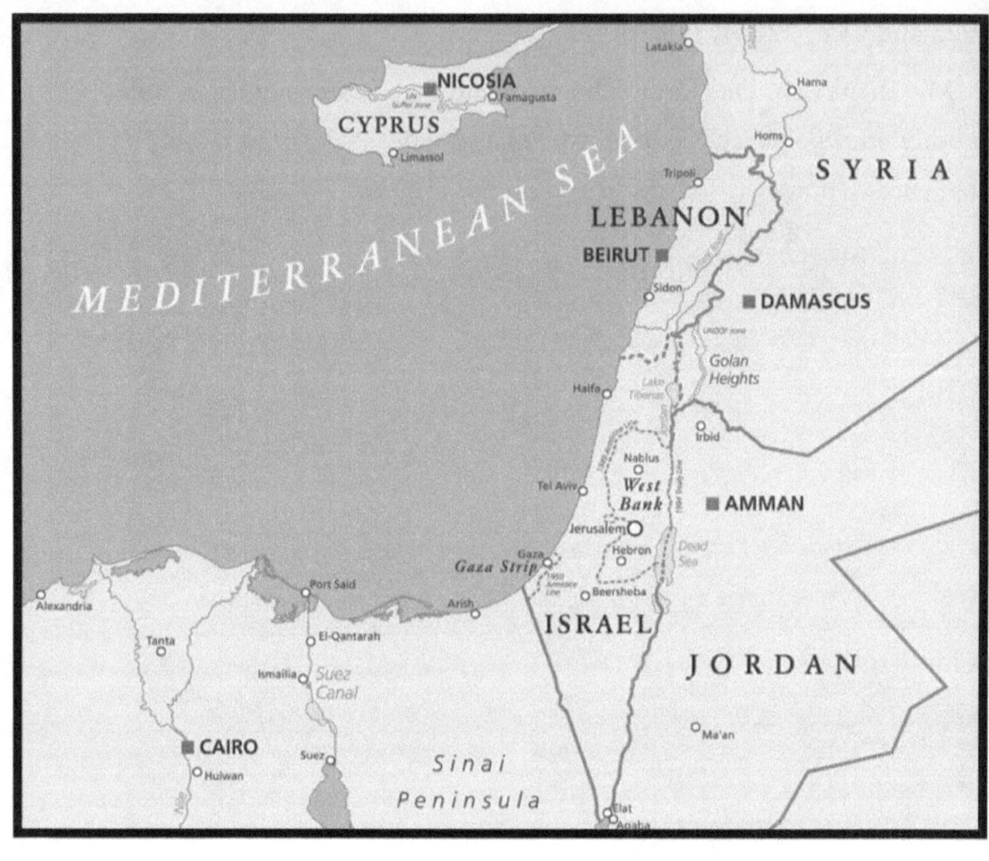

NICOSIA
CYPRUS
Famagusta
Limassol
Latakia
Hama
Homs
Tripoli
LEBANON
BEIRUT
Sidon
SYRIA
DAMASCUS
MEDITERRANEAN SEA
Golan
Heights
Haifa
Lake
Tiberias
Irbid
Nablus
Tel Aviv
West
Bank
AMMAN
Jerusalem
Hebron
Dead
Sea
Gaza
Gaza Strip
Beersheba
Alexandria
Port Said
Arish
ISRAEL
Tanta
El-Qantarah
JORDAN
Ismailia
Suez
Canal
Ma'an
CAIRO
Suez
Sinai
Peninsula
Hulwan
Nile
Elat
Aqaba

CHAPTER
ONE

THE VICTORY IN the Six-Day War amazed everyone. Israel was euphoric; the world was somewhat in disbelief that it took six days to decimate the Arab coalition of Egypt, Syria, Morocco, Iran, Jordan, and Lebanon. This war was only part of the ongoing Arab-Israeli conflict that included many battles and conflicts since the founding of the State of Israel in 1948.

During the Six-Day War of 1967, Israel had captured Egypt's Sinai, Syria's Golan Heights, and the territories of the West Bank which had been held by Jordan since 1948.The losses were catastrophic. Israel had in one week changed the map of The Middle East by now controlling 42,000 square miles. It now had 1.2 million Palestinians under its control.

In June 1967, shortly after the Six-Day War, the Israeli government voted to return the Sinai to Egypt and parts of the Golan Heights to Syria in exchange for a permanent peace settlement and admission of the return of the territories. Israel rejected the prospect of a mediated peace insisting on the need for direct negotiation with the Arab government. The situation became very clear in September 1967.

The Arab states had a post-war conference at the Khartoum Arab summit in The Sudan where they rejected any peaceful settlement with Israel. The eight participating states: Egypt, Syria, Jordan, Lebanon, Iraq, Algeria, and Sudan passed a resolution that become known as the 3 No's

1. No peace
2. No recognition

3. No negotiation

This was the state of the world that September morning when Michael Jannsen read those lead stories in the Boston Globe and the New York Times. There were a number of articles and he read them all. They covered the story from a variety of angles. He reached for the phone and called Benjamin "Bengy" Barak. Bengy was his fellow spy, partner, and dear friend who had lived through their clandestine ventures for the Mossad in Egypt and Iraq. All this was done to protect the State of Israel.

They had eliminated the V2 rockets that Nasser was planning to rain down on Tel Aviv. Their escape was a horrific experience that meant death if they were discovered. Michael's thoughts at the moment were reliving those memories. He was constantly rethinking the events and wondering whether he was ever going to escape what occurred. All of these ventures came to the foreground reading the headlines. He thought of Mr. Nsr, an Israeli spy who was part of Egyptian security staff. Without his help the missions would not have been successful. Mr. Nsr was the key person in their escape plan from Egypt. Michael was forever in his debt.

Doria walked in to the breakfast room. He hugged his wife; she was the love of his life and part of these experiences. She was the key person in the destruction of the V2 rockets. Her involvement allowed them to design a plan to destroy the rockets and the entire facility. They had fallen in love and Doria gave her allegiance to Israel by renouncing Nasser's policies of Israel's annihilation and his pan nationalism policies.

The call came through.

"Bengy, how the hell are you. What is going on with you and the boys?"

He was referring to Aaron Harel and Joshua Zanir who were the Mossad agents who orchestrated the operation they participated in. Both men were not only responsible for the plan, but devised their escape.

Bengy's first word was.

"I'm fine but…

"Let's get to them later, but first how is Doria, she must be due soon?"

Doria lost a child when she was viciously attacked by ex-Nazis in retaliation to Michael's destruction of the V2 rockets.

"Doria is fine and we are only two months away. She is right here. I will pass the phone to her."

Doria was so happy to hear his voice. Bengy was instrumental in saving Michael's life when he shot Hans Streiger, the Egyptian's munitions dealer who was about to kill him. Michael sought retribution for the loss of his child and the attempt on Doria's life. These events involved him in the espionage which was key to the success of the Six-Day War.

Bengy returned to their original conversation.

"Michael, I don't know what to tell you; Israel is still in a state of ecstasy over the results. Here in the Mossad, on the one hand, we are pleased with the outcome. On the other hand, we are concerned with the results of the Khartoum conference. If there are any significant changes I will be in touch. In the meantime, get ready to be a dad. By the way how is Greta?"

"She seems to be adjusting to a new country and will be a major asset to the company. We are fortunate to have her."

When he arrived in the office, he realized he had never spoken to Greta. With all the fire and fury, they had gone through, it was time to see how she was doing. He had her come to his office.

Greta Hirsh was a key factor in retrieving the V2 rocket blueprints and the limiting the threat of the Neo Nazi movement.

"I really am a little embarrassed that I have not spent the time with you. I was thinking about it this morning when I was speaking to Bengy. He sends his regards."

"Thanks, I am slightly overwhelmed with a new environment. America is so different than Europe. The job is exactly what I want. I just love the opportunity to develop new projects in your wonderful product center; it is a dream of a life time. This company has all the tools to build superb collections."

"You don't know how happy I am to hear your remarks. I am counting on you to be a creative force in this company. I realize you are not creative in sketching but your sense of style and merchandising is second to none. All you have to do is get to know our consumer's wants and needs."

"Enough about work, Michael said. "How are you doing personally? I realize you have been through hell. Being held for ransom for weeks had to be horrific."

"It's been difficult at times, the nights in particular. But it seems to be getting better. I have nightmares at times that Nazis are about to attack me for exposing them to the Israelis. I've found a great apartment in Brookline and you have arranged for a company car. Michael, I can't begin to thank you for all that you have done."

"Forget it, what you have done for the state of Israel, we can never repay. Do not hesitate if you need anything. You are a great asset to this company."

Michael had a business to run. It was no longer a mama and papa operation that Stone and Co. had started. It was now a major fashion operation with 125 stores nationwide but mainly in the eastern part of the country. There were four boutiques in Europe and about to grow.

Michael had grown into this business. Abe and Sarah, the owners saw the ability, creativity and drive in a 16-year-old son of Egyptian and Midwestern parents. They gave Michael the opportunity to become part of their business and life. They did not have any children and looked at him as if he were their son. He outperformed their wildest dreams with his creative, artistic ability and understanding of the market place.

He was not only able to communicate his ideas with sketches but he had that merchandising sense that few design people have. He used these skills to develop a "look" for Stone and Co. which women recognized as a way to dress. His concept of merchandizing and the ability to bring fresh collections to market on a regular basis made his customers loyal followers. His talent in design and merchandising coupled with a fantastic work ethic built the business.

He left for periods of time to fulfill his obligations to his heritage and protect his beliefs that Israel has a right to exist and flourish. Michael felt he had found a way to avenge the death of his dad at the hands of the Nazis. He was instrumental in defeating those who wanted to carry on the Third Reich. His work with the Mossad became a key factor in keeping Israel safe.

Armed hostilities continued on a limited scale after the Six-Day War. Israel began to settle the Golan Heights for they represented the greatest threat. They were determined the Golan would never return to Syria by placing settlements there, and the city of Jerusalem was reunited. Israel did not immediately try to settle the West Bank; the government policy was not to go beyond the "Green Line."

The Green Line was the armistice line of the 1948 Arab-Israeli war. It served as the de facto borders of the state of Israel and those of neighbors. Egypt, Jordan, Lebanon and Syria served as the boundary until the Six-Day War in 1967. The agreement represented Israel's internationally recognized borders with the two Palestinian territories: the West Bank and the Gaza strip. The Green Line was intended as a demarcation line rather than a permanent boarder.

Nasser's policy of the Three No's insured a perpetual state of war and essentially started the War of Attrition. Nasser sponsored Arafat from an early age and gave him the credibility to develop Fatah and terrorize Israel.

Nasser passed away on September 1970 and his successor Anwar Sadat explored the options for long term peace agreement with Israel. He was under pressure from the Egyptian street to restore Egypt's honor from its defeat in the Six-Day War. In addition, the Egyptian economy was in shambles, but Sadat knew deep reforms were needed and would be deeply unpopular among parts of the population. A peace initiative would not work politically.

The armistice agreements were clear at the Arabs' insistence that they were not creating permanent borders. The agreement covered Egypt, Jordan, and Syria. The Lebanon border was not covered and thus remained as before.

CHAPTER

TWO

MICHAEL WAS INTENT on expanding Stone and Co. using the talents of Greta Hirsh, who was the creative director of Kaufhaus, a German fashion chain of price sensitive fashion apparel.

Greta was directly involved in stifling the attempt of Neo-Nazi's to develop V2 rockets they wanted to rain down on Tel Aviv. She gave Michael and the Mossad the opportunity to discover the V2 rockets plans and the ability to destroy their organization. Michael and the Mossad were forever in her debt.

Greta became Michael's right hand in the creative and merchandising end of the business. Michael was still pondering whether she should be situated in Boston, or in Europe. He actually wanted her in both places. He needed not only her ability to work on her own but to be his sounding board for trends, ideas, and the normal issues of running a fashion business.

Abe and Sarah were the foundations of the business. They were now interested in stepping down from the everyday workings in the business. They felt Michael had all the tools to take over. They wanted to contribute but not on an everyday basis. Their interests were centered on their desire to spend time with family and soon-to-be adopted grandchild.

Doria was training personnel to expand her area. She was now running the administrative and logistical end of the business; she was in her seventh month of her pregnancy and working a full schedule. Doria was a finished product having overseen an international manufacturing and marketing operation in Egypt.

It seemed the three key people of Stone and Co had lives filled with intrigue, danger, and commitment to their ideals.

Michael was on his way to the product center that was about a football field away from the office complex. He made his way down to the facility a few times per day. Sometimes he was there late into the night developing the product line. On this trip he thought of his close encounter with death when the Neo-Nazi assassins tried to kill him. Thinking of the incident made him shudder. He was working on a new collection when the operator said Sir Arthur Brooks was on the line.

Sir Arthur was a "Sayan". The term in Hebrew meant helper. It was used by those who were willing to help Israel.

He had become an important link in helping Israel destroy its enemies. His family escaped Russia and settled in the UK, where he started selling clothes door to door. It was the start of Fantastique.

Sir Arthur owned the world's largest women's fashion business. Fantastique now had over 1500 stores throughout the world. He developed a different concept in retailing. His idea was to create the product from the initial sketch or concept to being placed on the racks. It gave him total control of every stage from development to the customer. Michael modeled many aspects of his operations after his organization.

Michael had worked a short time for Sir Arthur to establish a cover in his initial foray with the Mossad to destroy the Nasser V2 program. They became friends over a period of time. Sir Arthur continually wanted Michael to become part of his organization. They had the utmost respect for one another and Sir Arthur became a fatherly figure to Michael. Michael valued his friendship and was concerned they would be friendly competitors as Stone and Co. grew.

Michael picked up the phone and started the conversation.

"So how are you? I hope all is well with you and your family."

"Things are fine… and how is Doria and her upcoming bundle of joy."

They talked shop for a while and reminisced somewhat about their escapades together.

"Michael, I need to see you. It's rather important. When can you come to London? I will send my plane when your schedule is freed up. If you don't mind, I will send two of my design people to see your product center and you can come back with them. Let me know when you're ready. All the best."

Michael hung up the phone and was wondering what was on his mind. There was a sense of urgency in his voice. During the day Michael's thoughts were on the call. That evening during dinner, he brought up the subject with Doria. They were both wondering what had caused Sir Arthur to make this request

Greta was starting to get acclimated; she had gone through a horrific trauma being held hostage by German terrorists and held for ransom. She was on the verge of a total collapse when Michael and the Mossad rescued her. Greta was now in the States as part of Stone and Co. going through the learning curve.

1. Acclimating herself to Boston, MA from Dusseldorf, Germany

2. Learning new methods of the clothing business with a new company

3. Working with Michael.

It was a new Greta slimmed down from the ordeal. She had a sense of style and a level of sophistication in her appearance. She was now facing life in an entirely new environment. Greta was overjoyed with the opportunity to start a new life. She was in an excellent financial situation. Michael had arranged for the ransom payments which they confiscated to go to her. Michael was counting on her participation in her areas of expertise to expand the business.

Michael had not traveled since the episodes in Egypt and Germany, he had specifically wanted to spend time with his bride and rekindle the relationship. Her pregnancy made the decision so much easier for being supportive in every way.

Doria was an Egyptian beauty, statuesque, with deep blue eyes and olive skin. She carried herself with the grace of a fashion model even through her pregnancy. For Michael it was love at first sight. At that time, he did not know whether she was friend or foe. She worked for a notorious arms dealer who wanted to destroy Israel.

Michael's sandy skin color with deep penetrating eyes was mesmerizing. His six foot plus frame was sculptured from constant exercise. Both Michael and Doria stood out in a crowd.

It was somewhat of a surprise when Aaron and Joshua walked into Michael's office.

Michael was in the middle of a sketch.

"Please tell me you're here to see Doria and not for any other reason."

They all laughed

"We are here for a conference with our counterparts in Virginia. We thought coming to the states and not stopping to see your ugly face would be sacrilege. But we are really here to see Doria."

"How the hell are you?"

They spent an hour just catching up. Greta came in and they all spoke. There was a bond between them for they had all lived through the terror. They were now joined for life. Looking back at the past, they realized they were all there because each one did their part. That evening they all went to dinner at Taberna de Haro, drank three pitchers of sangria, and feasted on tapas and toasted to a hopeful new world. The following morning Aaron and Joshua met with Michael.

"I think we in Israel are in a state of euphoria over the results of the war. I imagine Bengy told you the same. We are left with the policy of the Arabs who have perpetuated the need of an endless struggle that translates into no peaceful settlement. There isn't any room for negotiation. In effect, Israel is locked itself into victory.

"The problem is we do not know what to do with this victory. In retrospect the Six-Day War has been a lost opportunity diplomatically, economically, socially, and even religiously. None of these dreams have come to fruition. They have given us a bitter sweet victory.

"Sadat reminds us daily that a state of war still exists. Most of the continued aggression takes place across the Suez Canal. His goal is to wear us down; this war of attrition being waged. Causalities are meaningless to them; for us it's a totally different story. To be honest there isn't a clear-cut policy or choice on the horizon. We contend with Fatah and Arafat on the points we just laid out. That's where we are. To be very honest I am deeply concerned the three No's no peace, no recognition, no negotiation are a recipe for a status quo at best."

Michael took it all in and thought about what he just heard.

"Is there any answer or are we just going to have to live our lives in constant readiness against these Arab states… ? Are we destined for a life filled with hatred for our neighbors?"

"I guess I better go back to designing the next collection and try to forget what I just heard."

Joshua ended the conversation;

"There's always hope."

CHAPTER

THREE

MICHAEL DID NOT say anything to the boys about Sir Arthur. He cleared a day for the Fantastique designers to come. He gave Sir Arthur the dates when he would be available.

The Fantastique's design staff arrived and Michael gave them the grand tour. They spent the day and both parties learned from the exchange. Michael was impressed with their knowledge of product and merchandising. The next morning, they flew on Fantastique's gulfstream to London City airport arriving at 7:45 pm.

There was a car waiting to take him to his favorite London hotel, The Connaught in Mayfair in the heart of the city. Michael thought he would spend an extra day shopping the fashion districts of London. The city was a key destination for seeing the newest in avant-garde fashion.

The next morning, he went to the Fantastique's office. Along the way, he had the cabbie stop so he could look at some fashion windows. Sir Arthur greeted him warmly and they sat down on the couch in his office. There was a magnificent view of the city all the way to the Thames. They had coffee and a wonderful English scone. There was some small talk of family and how Doria was progressing.

Sir Arthur then became quite serious;

"Michael I am about to take you into my confidence; no one knows what I'm about to tell you, not even my family. As you know my wife is deceased for quite some time and my only child died accidentally many years ago.

My closest living relatives are fine people but do not live in the world of business, let alone our world and the constant necessity to reinvent ourselves every quarter.

"I have been diagnosed with cancer, the kind you do not recover from. I probably have 6–8 months to live at the best of being productive."

Michael just sat there, not believing what he was hearing.

Sir Arthur continued. "I can see on your face that you are in disbelief, believe me, I had three separate opinions from the best of the best, all with the same diagnosis. So, the question is why did I ask you here?"

Sir Arthur got up and walked over to pour both some mineral water.

"Let me explain my thinking; this business has been my life. I've been at it since I was fifteen years old. I've dedicated all my efforts and resources to running this business. It was not only for my satisfaction but for the thousands of employees who work here and consider it home. You understand what I am saying because I know you run your business with the same dedication."

He caught his breath.

"I know if I decide to sell to some financial corporation or investment groups, they will without a question eventually destroy what I have built. They will first cut the staff and bring in their people that do not have any sense of running a fashion business. They will change the culture of the organization not for the better.

Wherever I'm going I can't fathom that I won't be constantly turning in my grave. I don't want to be ranting to the powers above on what is occurring under those conditions."

Michael smiled.

He was looking at a man who understood what it meant to be a "Mensch" in every sense of the word. He realized that if he was in his position he would be thinking along the same lines.

Sir Arthur went over to his desk and picked up a pad with a bunch of figures. Looked it over and put it down.

"I want you to take over this business. I realize what I am asking is difficult to equate at this moment. I only know of one person that I would trust with Fantastique, and that is Michael Jannsen. You have the know-how, the creativity, and integrity to continue this enterprise. I've seen you in action under numerous conditions. I've made it my business to find out just who you are. I've talked to the Israeli's, your competitors, your staff. You are that person."

Sir Arthur needed a moment.

"The question is, are you willing? If you are that man that I know you are, we will work out the problems and make this happen. I know how it can be done. I want you to think about my proposal. The means to get it done is really not the issue."

"I realize all the difficulties that are going through your head. That is not the main issue. You need time to think about what I just hit you over the head with. I want you to spend the rest of the day thinking about what could be and come back here tomorrow.

We will discuss how it will be done… I said will be done… not could be done! I know you are going to walk out of here and wander the city, the boutiques and Selfridge's. I know my customer."

Michael smiled.

"Think about doing it... Not the difficulties. Let's meet tomorrow morning and see where we are. I'm a very good judge of character."

Michael interrupted him.

"I certainly hope you are."

Sir Arthur smiled.

"Michael, remember when I first met you, you were in search of yourself, your past and heritage. You wanted to help our people and have a safe and secure life. I knew then you were that person of character. I knew my feelings were right then and more so now.

"Go... Shalom"

Michael left the office and as Sir Arthur said started window shopping every boutique and retail operation all the way to the hotel. He was looking at the product but his thoughts were with Sir Arthur. It took him two hours to navigate the boutiques; he finally ended up at Selfridges, probably the premier department store in the world. It was run more like a series of boutiques; every major designer or brand had a shop within the store. He spent two or more hours there and shopped not only all the apparel but the accessories areas including shoes and handbags. He was shopping for fashion trends and ideas. They took his mind off what was constantly churning in his head.

He wanted answers and the questions were repeating themselves as he walked through the shoe department. Michael finally made his way back to the hotel. It was almost six pm by the time he got to his room; he was mentally and physically exhausted from the meeting and the six to seven mile walk back. Michael threw off his sports coat and tie and picked up the phone to call the office.

It was midday in Boston when Doria answered.

"How are you? Did everything go well today?"

"Everything is fine. How are you feeling? You should not be working a full day at the store. You now have competent help."

"My meeting with Sir Arthur was quite interesting. We talked most of the morning and covered a number of subjects that pertained to each of our operations. I am being purposely vague because we haven't finished the issues under discussion. We are meeting again tomorrow and I will be able to give you definitive answers. I can't give you any more insight into what transpired until I finish up with him tomorrow. Can I talk to Greta and then Abe? Love you. See you soon."

He had a long conversation with Greta, over certain aspects of the new collection. He told her of some of the trends he saw on his voyage around London.

Abe and Michael discussed the merchandising of the key stores. In the trade they called them "A" stores. The sales figures were sensational and Michael was pleased. He briefly discussed Sir Arthur but nothings specific. Abe thought Michael went to London for a number of other issues.

Michael threw off his shoes and ordered room service; he was in no mood to go to the dining room. He turned on the TV, and before he could count to ten, he was in dreamland. It was always the reoccurring dream of being chased by Nasser. He was running as fast as he could with Bengy trailing behind him. He woke up fighting off the covers in a deep sweat.

Michael was up early and went to the fitness center and did his routine. He went back to the business center and sent telexes to the office. After breakfast he walked a few blocks and hailed a cab to Fantastique. He had no idea what he would say.

Sir Arthur started the conversation,

"So, where are we in this story? I presume both of us have thoughts on what should be done. I'm in a different position than you because my decision is based on events that I know are going to happen.

"On your level there are so many questions and problems that are floating around in your head; I feel badly that I have placed you into such a difficult situation."

Sir Arthur paused and thought about what he wanted to say.

"On the other hand, I know that you are that person that can lead Fantastique forward. You can use the power of this company not only to build it but to use its influence to make a better world. You have been battle tested for this position. It is becoming a very different world. My skills do not equate to what is needed in the future. They were quite adequate in my time, but not in yours. This new world demands leadership on a different level of expertise. I need to pass the baton to a person who can contend with the immense issues that he will face."

"Winston Churchill said it best.

'A man does what he must. In spite of personal consequences, in spite of obstacles and dangers and pressures, and that is the basis of all human morality.'

"That person is Michael Jannsen."

Sir Arthur caught his breath.

"Before you say anything, let me layout what I have in mind. Fantastique has approximately 1500 stores worldwide. The company is totally owned by myself.

There are no other stock holders. Our balance sheet is about as good as you can get. I've had the company valued by the best and many times over.

"This is what I am thinking,

"I will sell you Fantastique Ltd, for one pound or one dollar. All the profits are to be distributed as follows. 70 % of the new corporate entity which you will create is yours. 30 % will be divided to a group of charities, organizations, and the state of Israel. The profits from Stone and Co. are yours. That is not part of the 70%. This formula only holds true if there are profits. I will designate the percentages on the charities which I will list. I am over simplifying the process but in essence this is what I envision as the blueprint for the sale. My personal fortune which is not tied to the corporation will be distributed through my will and trusts."

"I would only present this offer to you for all the reasons I have just outlined. It's a lot to digest and I've been talking nonstop for a day and a half, I realize it's somewhat of a crazy idea, but not so crazy when you consider what is really meaningful for me and what I envision."

Michael sat there and tried to put it all together.

"Sir Arthur."

"Please call me Arthur."

"I am overwhelmed with your proposal. It's beyond my imagination that I am sitting here hearing what you outlined. I believe if I were in your situation with the same facts I would be thinking along the same lines. But I am not... The decision needs some deep thought and considerations such as family and obligations that I have entailed, I need to talk this through with my family."

"I understand your issues and more or less anticipated your answer, let's go about this at your pace. I need a decision shortly, but not today. Let me take you through our operation and our in-house design center.

"I have arranged for my plane to take you back later today or when you wish. If that works for you?"

Upon arriving in Boston, Michael didn't have any problems going through customs and immigration for he arrived on a private jet. It was incredibly convenient; the whole process took ten minutes.

When he arrived, Doria was waiting at the kitchen table. They caressed and after a quick rundown on how she was feeling, she wanted to know what happened in London.

"My Love… Sir Arthur is dying and wants to make sure that Fantastique will continue as is and continue to grow."

"He wants you to take over?"

"That's the situation. It seems incredible, like some kind of fairy tale. I believe I should explain it to you in Arabic."

"That's not necessary. What I want to know, are you serious? He actually wants you to take over his empire?"

"It's hard to believe but that's exactly what he wants."

"How can we possibly buy such a vast company? It must be worth at least a billion dollars."

"He wants to sell it to me for one dollar!"

CHAPTER

FOUR

In February of 1971, Sadat gave a speech to the Egyptian National Assembly outlining a proposal under which Israel would withdraw from the Suez Canal and the Sinai Peninsula along with other occupied Arab territories.

Jarring, a United Nations Swedish diplomat, made a similar proposal at the same time. Egypt responded by adapting much of Jarring's paper deferring on several issues and the Gaza Strip. This was the first time an Arab government has gone public declaring its readiness to sign a peace agreement with Israel. All the negotiations played out while Arafat and the Fatah organization were actively causing continued havoc. The Intifada was taking its toll.

Israel's Prime Minister Golda Meir reacted to the overture by forming a committee to examine the proposal and possible concessions. The United Nations unanimously concluded that Israel's interests would be served by full withdrawal to the internationally recognized lines dividing Israel from Egypt and Syria, returning the Gaza Strip, and, in a majority view, returning most of the West Bank and East Jerusalem, Meir was angered at the proposal and shelved the document.

The United States was infuriated by the response to Israel's response and Assistant Secretary of State for Near Eastern Affairs Joseph Sisco informed Israeli ambassador Yitzhak Rabin that "Israel would be regarded responsible for rejecting the best opportunity to reach peace since the establishment of the state." Israel responded to Jarring's plan on 26 February by outlining its readiness to make some form of withdrawal, while declaring it had no intention of the pre-5 June 1967 lines, which would nullify its gains in east Jerusalem and the West Bank. The Sinai was not the real issue.

Israel's ambassador to the UN, Abba Eban, told the Knesset that the pre-5 June 1967 which were the boundaries outlined after 1948 lines "cannot assure Israel against aggression"; Jarring was disappointed and blamed Israel for refusing to accept a complete pullout from the Sinai Peninsula.

Israel believed that the regional balance of power hinged on maintaining Israel's military dominance over Arab countries and that an Arab victory in the region would strengthen Soviet influence. Britain's position, on the other hand, was that war between the Arabs and Israelis would only be prevented by the implementation of United Nations Security Council resolution 242 and a return to the pre-1967 boundaries. Which Israel would never accept.

The political situation was tense as Michael reviewed his decision that had to be forthcoming, Sir Arthur needed to make his final plans no matter what he decided, and the decision could not be put off. He owed it to himself, the family and Sir Arthur. He discussed it with Abe and Sarah for these were key people in his life. He even sat down with his mother Hannah and told her the story. The decision was his. There were mitigating circumstances. Michael did not own Stone and Co. Would Abe and Sarah bless this opportunity to become part of a new venture? How would the new company be structured?

How would this be handled? Sir Arthur intimated that he envisioned a company within the company. How would that be achieved? There were a thousand questions to be answered. What it came down to was whether or not Michael Jannsen wanted to take on the responsibility and make life changing decisions.

As far as he was concerned the clock was ticking, and he could not avoid the need to finalize his thoughts and give Sir Arthur his answer. Sir Arthur insisted he send his plane for Michael. He called Sir Arthur to inform him that he was bringing Abe, Sarah, and Doria. She had insisted on coming even though she was almost due.

"The worst that can happen is to have the baby in London."

"Arthur, this is not only my decision but our families, we have worked together on every major issue, and it is the reason for our success."

"I understand, please bring them."

They all knew each other because of Michael's involvements.

Sir Arthur took over the meeting and explained how he thought the new corporation could function.

The financial elements were neither Michael's focus nor his real interest. His emphasis was on the creative, merchandizing ends of the business. Abe and Sarah's strengths were administrative and finance; actually, you could include Doria in that area since she ran an international business.

Sir Arthur was well prepared and laid out a momentary plan on the black board focusing on how both companies could operate independently and together at the same time.

The main point he made was that Stone and Co. would work independently within the Fantastique frame work. Arthur wanted all contracts to show that Michael Jannsen was the CEO and owner of Fantastique Ltd. He reiterated how he wanted the profits to be distributed. None of this was etched in stone and open for discussion except Michael's ownership.

The profits and liabilities of Stone and Co. were to be handled separately. How that was structured needed to be worked out by the financial teams. The financial aspects of the sale would take time. What Michael and Sarah wanted was a framework on how they would operate as two entities as one. They were open to what everyone thought. What they both assumed without any formal affirmation was that Michael had said yes. Actually, he did say yes by just showing up with his family. Only a train wreck could derail the melding of the two entities. Michael's head was filled with ideas on how the product lines would work; they could be used to the advantage of both.

On the broad outline that Sir Arthur laid out, it was necessary that all five parties sign off on these points. They discussed the points the rest of the day.

Abe led the conversation in the financial areas. Michael actually didn't say too much for he over the last two years had an intimate knowledge of Fantastique's abilities in design, manufacturing, merchandising, and retail. He was out of his league when the conversation centered in the financial and legal elements needed.

They were all talked out… it had been six to seven hours of non-stop conversation.

Michael asked Sir Arthur if he could have ten minutes with Abe, Sarah and Doria. Sir Arthur left them alone in the conference room.

"This is probably one of the biggest decisions, if not the biggest, I will ever make in my life. It's one that I cannot make alone. I need all of us to be on board. A unanimous decision is needed for me to go forward."

Michael hesitated as if he was thinking what he was about to say.

"I wouldn't be here if thought it could not be done. But that aside, I cannot do it or attempt it without all of you with me. I don't want you to say yes, just to placate me. I want you to vote based on your experience and belief. It can be done. There is a lot of money involved. This decision must be based not only on dollars and cents. It is one that demands the beliefs that we are carrying on a great tradition and fulfilling our dreams as well as Sir Arthur's. So, I am asking you to vote… one no vote and we will pass, what say ye?"

There wasn't a sound. They all looked at Michael and each one said yes.

"Shall we tell Sir Arthur?"

Michael and Doria flew home in Sir Arthur's plane. Abe and Sarah stayed and started a specific discussion on how they should proceed in the financial areas.

Michael was now interested in beefing up his Stone and Co. organization. He was extremely pleased that Greta was now part of the team. He felt she should play a significant role in the new corporation. Michael felt she would be able to become more than a second in command in the development and merchandising area. She had all the experience and qualifications. The question was what to do first? The approach Michael arrived at was to keep doing the same. Both entities were working well. Do not fix something that is not broken!! The new management program must be thought out and implemented in the proper manner over a period of time. In the meantime, it was business as usual.

CHAPTER
FIVE

Anwar Sadat came into office with an agenda. He was going to break the stale-mate and get back the Sinai by any means. He was quoted on saying that he was willing to lose one million men to achieve his ends. His first plan of action was to lobby the Soviet Union to help him with his plans. The Soviets thought little of Sadat's chances in any war. They warned that an attempt to cross the heavily fortified Suez Canal would insure massive losses. There were as many as25,000 Russian advisors engaged in Egypt. They were there to prepare the Egyptian army more than ever before.

The Israeli army on the other hand was suffering from underestimating the combination of these factors. The major point was the world became dependent on oil from the Middle East, and the Suez Canal was the key element.

Oil was inexpensive and controlled by the British and American companies. There wasn't a reason to develop fuel efficiency for the automobile or heating. The situation was ripe for price gouging and catering to the parties who controlled the supply.

The combination of Nasser's death, the rise of Arafat and the PLO, Israel's arrogance and the energy situation in the world, created the climate for what was to come. All of these elements came to fruition at one time. Nasser's death was a major economic blow to Egypt. Nasser was able to keep the economy on a reasonable basis. When Sadat assumed the leadership all belief in the economy fell apart.

Arafat arrived on the scene in the latter part of the 1950's and cofounded Fatah, a military organization which sought to replace Israel with a Palestine State. Fatah operated within several Arab countries from where it launched attacks on Israeli targets. In the 60's Arafat's profile grew and he joined the Palestinian Liberation Organization (PLO) and later was elected President.

He clashed with King Hussein and moved to Lebanon where he continued attacks on Israel although Nasser and his Arab allies were defeated in the war. Arafat and Fatah survived principally because they were the only option for the majority of Palestinians. They wanted to protect their only option… Fatah. Arafat was in conflict with Jordan and a constant threat to Israeli security.

These events set the stage for what was to become the War of Attrition.

This war Involved fighting between Egypt, Jordan and the Palestine Liberation Organization (P.L.O) and Israel following the Six Day War. A diplomatic resolution did not occur between the Arab League and Israel.

Nasser and the PLO believed that a continuation of a limited war and terrorist tactics would facilitate a full withdrawal from the Sinai. The PLO used these events to terrorize Israel's cities namely Tel Aviv.

Michael's thoughts were centered on two projects:

1 He needed a plan on how Stone and Co. would function with less involvement on his part.

2 How would he fit in as CEO of Fantastique?

This was a totally different problem for him. Sir Arthur was not the creative director but a shrewd and able leader spending his time in merchandising, finance, retail, and real-estate development. Many of these points were not his strengths. He needed to spend time with Sir Arthur and learn how he functioned.

He was concerned that the vastness of the new company would be way beyond Abe and Sarah's physical abilities. Running back and forth across the pond. He thought of his professors at Harvard business school, and who they would recommend to build up positions in this area. He also wanted to assess with Arthur how strong the candidates were in his organization.

There was another factor that weighted on him. He did not want to spend his life as an administrator or in finance or real estate. His strength and his desire were to create and merchandise the product lines. He did not want to spend his days in the other areas. There would be a need to find that person to fill those roles. Michael had to be the lead and the creative director of Fantastique Ltd.

He couldn't believe he was getting another call from Aaron and Joshua.

"What gives with you guys? I know you love me but aren't you taking this affair too far?"

"Michael. We heard you were possibly going to be in London next week or shortly after. We would like to run a few things by you."

"I really take my hats off to you. I thought you were magicians and soothsayers. Now I know it's true."

"Well, we are rather good at what we do. You know we are spies, but good ones.

You had to expect we would know. People come to us seeking information about you, if we told the parties just who you were."

There was laughter.

"Seriously, Congratulations. All the best. We do need to see you when you're there… let us know the schedule… Shalom."

That evening he reiterated the conversation to Doria.

"They are in a league by themselves. Don't ever sell them short. They always seem to know the next move no matter the situation."

"Michael, why do they want to see you? I Hope it's mostly a social visit."

"I don't believe it's entirely social; it's not their style knowing that we are about to enter into a whole new situation.

"There has to be a good reason for them to want to talk."

"I imagine you're right. We should know them by now. Somehow, they want or need something. We have to remember they live in an entirely different world than us. There's always a threat, a country, reason or organization that wants to harm Israel. It's a never-ending saga that keeps reinventing itself."

"Michael, I hope you're wrong."

"Maybe I am over reacting. I am still always on guard when I go anywhere. I carried a gun to London, just in case. It's a sad commentary of where we are in this crazy world."

Michael hugged her.

"We are about to have a wonderful child. I only hope his world will be better than what we have experienced.

"I wanted to talk a little shop with you before I head back to London."

"What would you like to discuss?"

"We have to plan for Abe and Sarah to have less involvement in their area. They will be needed in London for a short time for the merging of both entities. You and I cannot count on them carrying the ball independently. You must beef up your department and become available to oversee other areas, if necessary, at least for the initial stages."

"I realize this is doing double duty between baby and the business. I know we planned for help with the new born. This will be needed more than short term. I want you to analyze what you need for other administrative help and put it into action."

Michael spelled it out all in Arabic so there wouldn't be any misunderstandings.

"I am in full agreement. Actually, I have already started some of these administrative moves. I thought maybe you were ahead of me."

"I guess I was. We can speak English I completely understand."

They hugged one another.

The operator paged him and he went to the phone.

"Shalom." Both Aaron and Joshua were on the speaker phone.

"Both of us are going to be in London next week. We heard there was a possibility that you might be there."

Michael smiled.

"Is there anything you two thugs don't know?"

"Well, you have to remember a certain person came to us to find out who you really was. You have no idea what we told him."

"I bet you gave him a glowing report."

"Oh, we told him everything that we could think of and then some."

They started to chuckle.

"I can just imagine what you said."

"Seriously, if you're there next week we would like to spend some time with you. There are same possible issues and we would like to hear from an

Egyptian/Iraqi point of view."

"I will be there… you seem to know my plans before I do. I should have expected that."

"Send us a message when you firm up your plans. By the way congratulations!"

"Thank you but you have that ability to spook me… it scares the hell out of me."

They all laughed.

Michael was getting spoiled crossing the Atlantic in a private jet. It was the perfect way to travel. The Gulfstream had every convenience you could want. He was able to put in three to five hours of work during the trip and also rest.

He met with Abe and Sarah when he came to the Fantastique office. They had been there over a week and he wanted to hear from them how they were progressing.

"Michael, how is Doria, is everything proceeding as planned with the pregnancy?"

"She's fine and plans to work till the very last moment. I can't talk her out of it, taking time off."

"Tell me, how is everything going?"

The both of them started to talk at the same time and they started to laugh.

"Michael, we are totally pleased on what we have seen and Arthur's desire to make all information available to us. They have opened their books and given us all the information that we requested. Naturally we will have to bring in our financial people, but from all indications and my limited knowledge this company's balance sheet is triple A. I was very interested in their leases around the world, you won't believe this. Many of their "A" stores, they own the property. I do not know if that is part of the deal. Are they part of Arthur's estate or do they come along with the sale?"

Michael put his coffee down.

"I never thought nor dreamed that he owned store real estate."

"Would his estate be our land lord or is it part of the deal? How is it treated on the books?"

"I am not sure. It's up to Arthur; it is his call.

"I think it's time for us to discuss when we bring in the accountants and lawyers. I will have that conversation with Arthur today. It's entirely up to him when he wants to make this public. As far as I am concerned, I would prefer as late as possible, but whatever he wants."

Michael continued.

"So, as far as you are concerned from what you have seen, their business is about as good as it gets. I've been through their facilities a number of times and it seems to be state of the art."

Sarah interrupted.

"You can say we have a lot to learn on how to run a business from Fantastique. I have never seen a better run operation. Michael, they know trends and sales numbers that will make our system child's play. Their system will give us a world of information."

"I guess I'm getting the feeling that we need them to improve our own business."

"It seems that way."

Sir Arthur Walked into the conference room.

Michael said, "Arthur, how are you feeling. I want you to know that we are honored that you chose us to continue this wonderful company. My main purpose for coming is to tell you that I want to make the transition as easy as possible. Whatever and whenever you want done, that's what will happen. Personally, I am humbled to be chosen to run the business. I will forever be grateful to you for giving us the opportunity to be part of what you have built. We will not let you down; it will flourish and grow as if you were here."

Arthur got up from his desk and hugged him.

"Michael, I know I chose the right person and know you will make me proud. I am so pleased that you and your family agreed to make Fantastique part of your lives. I can rest easy knowing it's in good hands. My greatest fears have been set aside by your decision. I can't thank your enough."

Michael did not bring up any questions nor did he ask for any information. His mission was to tell Arthur how he felt. It would be up to him to decide on the schedule. The timetable was his alone. Abe and Sarah would continue their learning about the company's workings in their areas of expertise. Michael had seen and knew the capabilities of product development and merchandising the collection. The deal had what we call rhythm… Michael still couldn't believe it was happening.

Michael met Aaron and Joshua in one of the Fantastique conference rooms. It was like old times meeting them when they strategized the destruction of the V2 rockets that Streiger the German/Egyptian had developed with Nasser to reign down on Tel Aviv.

"So why are we here? I am happy to see your ugly faces. So, let's have it, the truth or the real story."

CHAPTER

SIX

Joshua spoke first.

"We wanted you to hear what we are concerned about. As of this moment there is nothing concrete but it's our job to look down the road and not only see what is there but what's beyond that hill.

"We are worried and like I said earlier, Israel is still in a state of ecstasy over the victory. The army is feeling its oats and I don't think paying enough attention to what is happening in this War of Attrition that Arafat is waging. It's difficult to get the parties to be on tract when they are feasting on yesterday's wins. Maybe we are being too suspicious but that's our job. We wanted your opinion on certain situations and possible solutions. We realize you're about to enter in to a whole new business which will make you a difficult person to reach. We wanted to bother you now, rather than later."

Michael started to smile.

"I'm happy that you are so concerned with my schedule, seems the story of my life is that every time I turn around you seem to be there. I'm not complaining, I've given up on that score. How can I possibly help?"

Aaron then opened the discussion.

"Let me give you a little background so you will understand the complete picture. The Arabs have given us an eviction notice of the Three No's.

No peace

No recognition

"They are carrying on a War of Attrition with the main threat being Arafat/Fatah and causing significant problems on the West Bank and Jordan."

"Sadat is having his troubles at home. All their actions show they are wanting war. The years since he has taken office, he has thrown the nation into chaos. Confrontation has become a desperate option. The drums of war are starting to beat much louder than yesterday. We believe he's desperate and even willing to go to war without Soviet support. We can see the starting of a buildup of their forces receiving all types of jet fighters, anti-aircraft missiles, tanks, guided missiles from the Soviets. Not only weapons but Russian personnel in Egypt for training and improving military tactics.

"They are replacing political generals who had in a large part been responsible for the rout in 1967. They replaced them with competent ones. All these events lead us to one conclusion; war is imminent. We do not believe we are over estimating the opponent or the situation. Our problem is we may be resting on our laurels."

Michael sat there for a moment.

"Guys- Bengy and I are not going back to the Egyptian airfields to find out their strengths and I am not blowing up anymore rockets. So, what do you want from me?"

Joshua continued.

"We understand you're not going back. We need you to offer some insight into how we should proceed. Let me give you the background."

The U.N. Security Council after the Six-Day War proposed an agreement that there was a policy from Egypt that could bring about a peace treaty with Israel. The U.N. concluded that Israel would be served by a full withdrawal to the internationally recognized lines dividing Israel from Egypt and Syria, and returning the Gaza Strip. It also wanted returning most of the West Bank to Jordan and East Jerusalem. Golda Meir rejected the proposal out right.

The United States was infuriated by the response of the Israelis answer to the Egyptian proposal. They were ready to curtail weapon shipments. Israel responded to The U.N. plan by out-lining its willingness to make some form of withdrawal while declaring that it would not return to the pre-June 5th 1967 lines.

"As you know, they ended up giving back most of the Sinai and the Gaza Strip. What this brought about was that Britain and especially France decided not to sell weapons of any sort to Israel. Britain kind of looked the other way but France specifically set up deep constraints. We are exceptionally dependent on France for particular weaponry, mainly the Mirage III and its parts. It is now a major problem.

We know that France whether through legitimate sources or black-market munitions dealers have sold weapons to Hans Strieger, the munitions dealer who developed the V2 rockets. We must find the means to achieve our goal of acquiring the weapons no matter what it takes. Many of the contacts that make these deals are brokered through parties who are from the Middle East.

Michael interrupted vehemently.

"Guys… find someone else, how many times can I roll the dice without crapping out!"

"We understand, I'm telling you what we think we need to get what we need. We must finalize a plan."

Michael joined Sir Arthur in his office after seeing Aaron and Joshua off. He had mixed emotions every time they met. They had gone through so much together. Their lives and many others hung in the balance on their actions; they would be forever bonded with each other.

He was thinking of what they had said. It did not equate well. His sixth sense was starting to work in overdrive as he reviewed the points they had made. He couldn't help thinking that once again he would be involved. He started to feel the clock ticking toward confrontation. Michael tried to put it out of his mind as he sat down with Arthur.

Arthur started the conversation.

"I see your buddies were here. I hope it was a social visit."

"Arthur, you know them too well. It's never a social visit."

They both laughed.

Michael wanted to explain.

"Israel is never without the real possibility of a new conflict on the horizon. It's their responsibility to be on guard on every possible issue that could bring conflict. They had asked me what I thought about the events since the 67 War."

Sir Arthur answered,

"I wouldn't have done anything differently. They would not have performed their duty without speaking to you."

"You're probably right"

"Let's talk about us.

There is more to running this business than all the normal areas you have experienced in the States. This is the United Kingdom not Boston, Massachusetts."

"You do not need any tutoring in making this business function. You have all the tools, actually more than I ever had. What I need to teach you is how to function in the nasty political climate of England. We are going to start the learning curve by meeting some of the key people that run this poorly run country. They are pompous, many not qualified and Anti-Semitic. The problem is you have to live with them. If you do not, they will destroy you. I am over stating the situation so that you will understand the need to be a political person."

"There are many elements that need to be addressed and I will make you aware of them. We are going to start your education over lunch with some of these people. You have to remember that I am Sir Arthur Brooks, knighted by the Queen, not because I built Fantastique, but for my involvements in politics and charity work."

"You are now going to be put in situations that you haven't experienced. I know that you are well aware of some of our British points of view. But living with them on a daily basis is quite different. I know how you "hood winked" Nasser. This country and people are unique and you need to learn the rules and how they work."

"This is a horse of a different color as you would say; the emersion in English politics unfortunately can't be helped. I am not going to try to give you the history, but there are a few things you should know before we meet some of the people that run this country. I will give you some information that has affected me in some ways. We have a number of retail stores in Northern Island; I have been involved with a group that has tried to mediate the problems."

"In 1969 James Caunghan, Labor's foreign secretary took a decision to send the British army to Northern Ireland to keep the peace. At first the troops were welcomed by the Catholic community residents. The happy relationship was not to last. The IRA which had been dormant reorganized itself and took the lead in the struggle. It helped the Catholic Nationalist Party and targeted British troops in Northern Ireland. They were the hated British Imperialistic government that caused all of Ireland's problems.

When the current conservative party came in, the violence convinced Edward Heath, who is the current prime minister to further action. Ruling went in force for the Internment Act, arresting suspected trouble makers and holding them without trial. They thought this method would reduce sectarian tensions. It had the opposite effect. The results were,

1. Increased tension in Northern Island.
2. A feeling among Catholics that they were being persecuted.
3. Strained relations between Irish government in Dublin and London.
4. Political strife between labor and the conservative parties.

I've given you this small piece of British politics because I have been involved. I find myself in the middle, which has both sides not very happy. We are going to meet some of these players as you say on your side of The Pond tomorrow for lunch. I've put together some articles that you can read over this evening so that you will be aware of what a mess we are in."

Arthur paused,

"Let's talk about this business"

Arthur started to take Michael through his three-year plan that he put together before he knew of his diagnosis.

"Michael, I don't know it if fits with your ideas. I want you to study it and see what you like and dislike. I would like you to analyze how we should go about keeping our stores new and exciting. Not only through new merchandise but also to keep them enticing in every way. We shall look at some of the plans for refurbishing and prototypes for new openings. You have your homework... I'll see you in the morning. Oh, suit and tie, we are going to an exclusive club."

"By the way, Abe and Sarah have asked the right questions and I am impressed with their knowledge in many areas".

"Arthur… they built Stone and Co. I just furthered what they started."

Abe, Sarah, and Michael met for dinner. They really hadn't spent much time with one another in the last weeks. They ate at the Connaught. There were very few in the dining room.

"So what did the two of you find that I should know?"

"Everything and nothing"

They all laughed.

"Actually, that's true, their overall operation seems to function very well at every level. The problem is that it's a very big ship and it takes time to change course if necessary."

"What I mean is they have a plan and when it is working, it is something to behold. It's really impressive.

"Where is the glitch?"

"It takes time to correct what is not working. The whole idea is to find ways to make that big ship turn faster if there was an issue. They are brilliant in other areas. You notice I said brilliant; it's the British word for good."

They all laughed.

"Abe, you're about the best merchant that ever lived. What are they missing?"

"I know they can do much better in the accessories area such as footwear and handbags. It is not so much what they have; it is what they don't have, which is a wider variety of product and additional styling."

"Enough, let's eat… !"

Michael had his reading assignments but first he wanted to speak to Doria and Greta. He spoke for over thirty minutes with Greta about the entire collection. She must have been wondering why there were all in London but didn't say anything to Michael.

He finally got to Doria,

"How are you, my love? How are you feeling?"

"Michael, I feel our baby kicking, I am in seventh heaven."

"Please take care."

Have you found some additional help since we talked?"

"We are working on it. I think we found someone that fits into our system."

"How's my mother and sister, I owe them calls. Let's make plans to take them to dinner."

"I've seen them—they are fine."

Michael opened the manila envelope from Arthur and started reading. He became so involved that when he looked at the clock… It was two am.

Just one more paragraph, he thought.

"The IRA, The Irish republican army is dedicated to the creation through violence of an all-Ireland republic. Its political front was Sinn Fein a legitimate political party. In 1969 the movement split into the official IRA and the provisional IRA.

He laid out his Armani suit, shirt and tie along with his Italian dress shoes. He also packed his Glock pistol with an extra clip. After the two incidents in Boston and Dusseldorf he didn't go anywhere without his weapon. He had been trained by the Mossad and practiced ever since.

Michael tried to access the reading material in real terms. Arthur was right. This was an entirely different situation that he faced. There were local Boston politics that he had to address but nothing on the scale that he would have to face in the U.K.

This situation with the IRA That Arthur had outlined could be a serious issue. He was going to make it a priority to know how it could affect Fantastique and his family. The warning signs could be there.

The next morning, Arthur gave him a quick rundown on the group he was about to meet.

"We are lunching at White's which was founded in 1693 in St. James. It is quite exclusive as you can imagine.

"We have to look into getting you a membership. I can vouch for you as a member of good standing."

They laughed.

"There will be some influential people who you should be aware of. You notice I said people not friends; I'm not sure how many would attend. They will want to know all about you, so tell them. You're very good at selling yourself."

"You are sure to meet Selwyn Lloyd who is the leader of the House of Lords. You probably know the name Edward Heath who is the Prime Minister. They have no idea of my situation. What they know is you are my designated successor as I approach retirement. They will know when it is the right time."

CHAPTER

SEVEN

THEY WENT DOWN to the garage and Johnson his driver and handyman pulled the Bentley up, Michael was slightly in awe with this magnificent automobile. He had seen so few. He couldn't see the difference between a Rolls or a Bentley.

The ride to White's took about 20 minutes. When they arrived, Michael was impressed with the building before him of 276 years old.

It was pomp and circumstance when you enter the club. The staff was attired in tails with white gloves. Michael was thinking this only happens in the U.K. Naturally there was a private dining room. It was furnished in dark mahogany furniture. Every piece shined under the chandelier.

They were slightly early and waited for the guests, and the expected group. It turned out to only be two. It seems there was a mix-up in schedules. The two that arrived were the key people, Selwyn Lloyd was the speaker in the House of Lords. Edward Heath was the Prime Minister. They were all seated after introductions and Sir Arthur started to officially introduce Michael.

"As you know I am making my plans for retirement… and that has brought up the subject of succession for the leadership of Fantastique Ltd. The search for my successor did not take long for I have known him for a number of years. He has proven to me that he is not only capable of leadership, he has the ability to take Fantastique to the next level and beyond. On this bass I have made my decision and he is here, so all of you can get to know him. Let's welcome him to England here is Michael Jannsen."

There was a round of applause and Michael rose to speak.

"Gentlemen I can't tell you how honored I am to be chosen to continue the leadership of Fantastique Ltd, after Sir Arthur's retirement. I know that all of you have the utmost respect for Sir Arthur and his commitment not only to Fantastique but his allegiance and dedication to the United Kingdom. He has proven that over the years when it counted. I hope in my own way as someone coming from colonies."

There was laughter,

"I will carry on his tradition of not only using Fantastique as a business venture, but to use its resources for the good of the British Empire and its subjects."

There was applause.

They were all talking at once and asking questions when they yielded to Edward Heath.

"Mr. Jannsen, your words were well spoken. I am extremely pleased that you were chosen for the leadership of Fantastique. You were correct; the company is more than just a retail entity. It was born and nurtured in the U.K. before it spread its wings around the world. Even though you are from the colonies, I know you will continue its ideals."

There were chuckles and applause,

They had their six-course lunch and continued the conversation into the early afternoon.

Michael could see that Sir Arthur was very pleased with the course of events.

As soon as Michael, Sir Arthur with Lloyd and Heath exited, the club his sixth sense and Mossad training kicked in.

Standing on the entrance steps he immediately realized it was too quiet and the two security guards attached to the prime minister were nowhere to be found.

The guards had been at the back or the room throughout the luncheon, where were they? Michael's thoughts were flashes of what he read the previous evening. This could be an attack on the Prime Minister by the IRA, The provisional IRA. It triggered Michael's sense of danger, survival mode, and action.

They had arrived in two cars, the prime minister with the speaker and Michael and Sir Arthur. The two Bentleys were there waiting for their occupants. Both chauffeurs were standing with doors open.

Michael was decisive.

"Gentlemen, please do what I say. All of you get in the car as soon as possible." He actually started pushing them in and down on the floor.

Johnson was at the door. He pushed him aside slammed the door and jumped into the driver's seat. The Bentley was the standard right-hand drive of the UK. If it was an American vehicle, it would have been much more difficult to enter. He would have had to enter from the other side and be exposed to the potential terrorists. The car was actually running when Michael jumped in and immediately brought it forward. He realized the terrorists were primarily interested in kidnapping the Prime Minister; otherwise, there would have been gunfire.

He threw the Bentley into reverse, but was not able to go very far because of the parked cars. He tried giving himself a little more room.

He drove the vehicle up on the sidewalk and tried to maneuver around the blockage. He had drawn his gun and had it on his lap, ready to fire when and if the terrorists appeared to fire.

Michael knew there was only one course of action before gunfire would start. He backed up as far as he could and floored the accelerator and rammed the blocking vehicle.

He caught them by surprise for they didn't have a chance to move their vehicle to lessen the collision or escape the blow. Their autos were not the size or weight of the Bentley; the body was steel and aluminum and much stronger than the cars they rammed. Michael again backed and rammed the other car. There wasn't a sound from the back. On the second attempt he had opened up some space and the possibility of getting through the wider opening. Michael again told his passengers to keep their heads down and brace themselves for the coming impact.

With more room to maneuver, Michael brought the Bentley around and in reverse rammed the vehicle. Michael was now worried, how long are they going to wait before they move in and start a firefight. It seemed their original plan was to pull off the kidnapping without gunfire. He believed Heath's security people were in on the plot. He had to react now or they would be in serious trouble. The Bentley was starting to throw off smoke and he believed it was about to lose power.

Michael needed either a miracle or a diversion that would cause them to stop the coming assault and cover their escape. He thought… Water… the destruction of the water towers in Nasser's missile complex was the means they used to destroy the facility and escape. Michael backed up the Bentley with as much speed as he could muster and slammed into the water hydrant located alongside the building causing cascading water flooding the street and the terrorists' cars. Actually, there were very few people in this area. It was mostly an area with club and private residences. The gushing water forced whoever was there to move away from the scene.

The terrorists in their damaged vehicles did not attempt anything further. They were more interested in fleeing and not being apprehended. Somehow or another the damaged Bentley was still durable. There were few pedestrians just starting to gather as they departed. The passengers were still in shock. They slowly realized they were now safe and Michael drove away. Michael went directly to Sir Arthur's residence in Mayfair.

Heath was the first to speak,

"This incident did not happen; there was a terrible accident at St. James with a number of vehicles colliding which set off the water works flowing in the streets. Our assailants will say nothing for their mission was a failure and they will be embarrassed to their comrades. I want these series of car crashes to be just what they were. More than likely some of the drivers were intoxicated which led to the mishaps. I will now have this incident reported to the police and the press on that basis. There haven't been any casualties which is reason to find this situation never happened."

Michael had driven to Sir Arthur's home. Heath went straight to the phone and spoke to the parties who would put his plan in place.

"Mr. Jannsen, I thought you were quite capable and wise when you spoke over lunch I did not realize when I spoke my words that you were living proof of them. I thank you for myself and England. You saved us from a very difficult position."

Sir Arthur embraced Michael.

"You are all and more than I thought. I know I can rest easy. I can't tell you how proud I am of you."

On page six of the evening London Times was an article describing the spectacular accident involving three automobiles. The article went on to relate that the accidents occurred in the Saint James area, and set off the water works flooding the street. It was reported that no one was seriously injured. Michael wanted to go home. Doria was always on his mind and he wanted to be there when the baby was born.

Time was running short and he needed to layout programs with Greta to see the new prototypes that were being developed. He decided not to tell Abe and Sarah about the incident. They didn't need to be upset. He definitely wasn't telling Doria.

Abe and Sarah had reached a point in their discovery where the professionals had to take over the legal and financial groups and both sides had to finalize the agreement. They all went back on Sir Arthur's jet.

CHAPTER

EIGHT

GRETA CAME TO Michael's office and they discussed the line development. When they had finished all the points, she had some issues.

"Michae, I still have a lot of affairs in Germany that have not been settled, I have a safety deposit box that needs to be emptied and a condominium and a car that needs to be deposed of. Is it possible that I could take a week to ten days to get these things done?"

"When do you want to go?"

"When you think is right for you. I don't want to hold up any projects."

"Greta, it's never the right time. We are always busy. It's best that you go now since we have Ninety Eight percent of the product line in the development cycle."

"Michael, I am afraid to go alone. Could you arrange for someone to be there with me?"

"I understand perfectly. Let me see what I can do to arrange that you have security."

Michael called Bengy.

"I know you have people stationed in Germany. Greta has not been back since the incident. She needs someone to watch over her while she cleans up her personal effects. Is it possible for you to arrange something? This is the least we can do for what she has lived through for us."

"I'll get it done. She actually knows Yakov who was there to help you and Greta."

All this occurred when Michael and the Mossad had devised plans to destroy the Aryan Party and fold any efforts to rebuild the V2 rocket program.

The Aryan National Party had lost two of their key members, Herr Adler and Herr Schneider, in a confrontation with Elsa Goering of the R.A.F., a radial German terrorist organization. There was a fire fight over the abduction of Greta Hirsh. The two members of the Neo-Nazi movement were killed during the incident.

They also lost the would-be assassin who botched the killing of Michael Jannsen and Greta. Alder's son Heinz who was working with Greta was out for revenge. He blamed her for his father's death.

Greta had known the key members in the organization. She and Adler were lovers and she attended many of their functions. She was able to give the Mossad a list of the council members. Greta was not only a threat to their identities but a traitor to the cause. When she disappeared with Michael they tried to find her to no avail. They reached the condominium association and asked them to contact them if she reappeared. When Greta arrived in Dusseldorf to finalize her affairs she decided to stay in a hotel. She was afraid to go to her apartment alone.

Michael had organized a program that Greta would contact the Mossad agent in Germany and work out a schedule. She was extremely nervous without someone by her side. Greta got up enough courage to go to the bank alone. This is where she had been taken hostage by Elsa Goering, the leader of the R.A.F. German terrorist organization.

She opened her safe deposit box and went through her papers as well as her jewelry. It took her sometime to sort everything out. She even found some papers her brother had given her before he died in Iraq. She opened them and saw there were lists of Neo-Nazis that he and Hans Streiger had helped through the Odessa to escape to South America and the Middle East. She closed the list quickly and would pass it on to the Mossad agent.

Before she left for the trip, Michael had her buy a Glock pistol, the smallest model that would fit in her purse. He sent her for lessons four to five times before her trip.

The Aryan National Party had members who worked at the bank. When Greta appeared, they notified the powers to be. The decision was to have her eliminated. They would try to make it accidental if possible.

She contacted a real-estate person to place the condominium on the market. Greta only wanted to take her personal belonging and leave Germany as soon as possible.

Greta had contacted Yakov and wanted him to accompany her to the condominium. She was not going to go by herself no matter what. When the association was notified of Greta's intentions they called Herr Gruder of the Aryan party. They already knew she was here through their banking connections. They devised a plan and contacted Herr Adler's son Heinz who had worked with Greta. He had blamed Greta for his father's death and wanted revenge. Greta and Yakov arranged a date to remove her belongings. They purposely informed the association they would be arriving on a specific day. This information was conveyed to Gruder who put his plan in effect.

Actually, they were planning to come the previous evening to avoid any problems with anyone appearing that had any plans to hurt Greta. Heinz had put a vigil on her residence days before. He did not see them enter for he had gone to dinner. When he saw the lights on when he returned, he rushed up to the apartment knife in hand. Yakov stepped in front of Greta and smashed Heinz's leg and in two moves he was moaning on the floor.

Greta was shaking as they left with her suitcases. Yakov was ready for Heinz, for his comrade sat in the car and radioed him of Heinz's arrival. When Greta filled out the paperwork for the sale of the condominium she had to list her personal address.

When Herr Gruder received the information, he was angry that they had been out foxed, however they now knew where Greta was living and where Michael was located. They wanted to avenge their comrades and the V2 rocket fiasco.

Michael's part in the formation of the new corporation was now limited. It was in the hands of the lawyers and accountants. Abe would oversee this section of the agreement. They had excellent legal staff with the finest Boston law firm for their own needs. Michael flew across the Atlantic once again to work out the merging of many elements of their product development facilities. It needed some specific answers that only he, Arthur and his product development chief could answer. The meeting had to cover specific details on how they could work together and remain autonomous. They wanted Stone and Co. to maintain its individuality in the new company. Aaron and Joshua showed up at their door. This time there was a serious look on their faces. There were few pleasantries. They came to see both Michael and Arthur.

Joshua started the conversation.

"Gentlemen, we are in a very difficult situation and we believe you can help. Let me give you some background so you understand the issue. We are certain war is coming. The rest of Israel may not be on the same page for a variety of reasons but we and many in the I.D.F. (Israel Defense Force), are extremely concerned because of the inability at this time to be prepared for an armed conflict. Our problem is centered around the inability to acquire specific weaponry because of the embargo's placed on by certain nations, primarily Britain and France. We need your help to acquire this weaponry. It will need methods that can only be done by private enterprise."

Michael interrupted.

"Guys, I thought Israel had developed sources that were delivering the lion's share of the IDF's (Israel Defense Force) weapon systems in house."

"That is true… but many of the essential parts come from outside which has placed us in a difficult position. On top of that key pieces are still totally dependent on Britain and mainly France. Over the years the Israeli government did not want to subsidize the arms industry to that extent. It felt it had too much power and has looked at the industry in a different light then it did before the Sixth Day War."

Aaron continued the conversation.

"We pissed off the French so we can't kiss and makeup under any conditions."

"What caused this situation?"

"The Cherbourg Project was an Israeli military program to develop a new small missile boat. They were made by the French and paid for by the Israel government. They were not delivered due to the French arms embargo in 1969. De Gaulle was adamant and would not release the boats. There was pressure from the Arab League.

The Israelis using the Mossad "arranged" to have the boats sold to a straw company. They secretly brought Israeli sailors to Cherbourg and sailed the boat to Israel which was quite a feat. You can imagine the up roar and De Gaulle was incensed. We have to use the munitions dealers; we do not have a choice."

Joshua picked up the conversation.

"Michael, I don't have to tell you about private arms sales after your dealings with Hans Streiger and Nasser. It's a nasty business. Unfortunately, we feel it's a way out of this mess. We are about to have to deal in this area to gain the necessary weaponry that we need. We need the both of you. Michael's ability to speak two dialects of Arabic and Sir Arthur's reputation and influence are the pieces we need to put the scheme into effect. We have devised a plan which I want to layout for you both. I realize what we are asking at this time, but we really do not have another alternative."

Michael got up and walked around the table.

"So, what did you come up with?"

"Give me a few minutes to give you the background so you will know why we are here.

"In the early 1950's, France and Israel maintained close political and military ties. France was Israel's main weapons supplier until the French withdrawal from Algeria in 1962 three days before the outbreak of the 6 Day War. Charles de Gaulle imposed an arms embargo on the region mostly affecting Israel. The embargo has severely limited our long-term strategy, planning, and capability. It caused a shortage in spare parts for most of Israel's French Aircraft. At start of the 6 Day War France was forced to pick a side. In a shock to all, they chose the Arab states, despite aggressive moves by Egypt. In 1969 de Gaulle retired and we hoped the new president Georges Pompidou would lift the weapons embargo. He did not and this is where we are today."

"On an additional issue in 1970 a near civil war broke out between Jordan and Arafat. He and his organization were expelled from Jordan. Syria sided with the PLO and even helped it militarily. Jordan did not feel comfortable joining the Egyptian-Syrian alliance. Iraq refused to join in on an attack, Lebanon did not want to get involved because its army was small and unstable. With all these factors in play, Sadat was set on war. We know that he had secret meetings to prepare for a conflict."

"In 1971 keeping even the higher-level commanders in the dark he planned to attack Israel in concert with Syria. The code name for the operation was "Badr" after the battle of Badr in which the Muslims defended the tribes of Mecca. We know all this because of our mutual friend Mr. Nsr who is in the Egyptian secret service but a spy for Israel. The embers of conflict were burning brighter and hotter."

Sir Arthur interrupted the conversation.

"Why don't we move against them now?"

"Good question. You know some of the answers… complacency, ecstasy over the victory and the decision not to initiate a war. We did not want to alienate our relationships with the west especially the United States."

Michael had heard enough.

"Let's get to the nitty gritty on how we can get you the weapons you need"

"Michael, France is the key. The majority of what we need comes from them. There are a number of munitions dealers, but we are concentrating our efforts in finding the person who has the equipment that we need.

Our plan is not completed as of the moment"

Michael looked at them. Why?

"We want an Iraqi arms dealer to purchase a black-market group of weapons from Western Europe, mainly Britain and France. These weapons are supposedly destined for the Kurds who as you know are constantly at war with Iraq and also have regular customers in Africa. You know firsthand of the Peshmerga Kurds rebels who killed Schmidt in Iraq and only by luck did not kill Bengy. As you already presumed you are the Iraqi dealer that will buy the goods."

"Michael, we are using the same format that was successful in Egypt. With the necessary twists we will need to invent the Iraqi and a history. It will mean going to Iraq; unfortunately, we cannot avoid that. We are planning this should be done in two to three weeks, or less."

"We have already spent time inventing this person. His name is Jamil Abbas. He is your age with a wife and family living in Baghdad with a mistress. He has been a trader in illicit goods on an international basis and has a large warehouse in Baghdad and in the north of Iraq with all types of goods including military weapons bought on the black market. Mr. Abbas has a sophisticated organization with several key English ex pats living in Baghdad, his weapon inventory consists of items from the U.K., the U.S. and France. This is a quick rundown on how this will work. We will use Sir Arthur to contact him in France. All the details will be worked out with Sir Arthur, who will have him contact you. In essence this is the plan we will use to make the connection, his customers are Iraq and Iran, who are not able to buy French Munitions because of the embargo."

Michael sat there for a moment taking it all in.

"If I say yes… you already know I will say yes; I can't refuse you. When will this plan be put into operation?"

"As soon as you can come to Israel, for three days and get things started. We want this done as soon as possible."

Arthur entered the conversation,

"What do you want of me?"

"We will give you the program when Michael will be in Tel Aviv, one of our people along with Joshua or myself will fill you in."

Michael wanted to make it very clear.

"You have to realize if Doria has complications or the baby is early, I will have to postpone this operation. Right now, she is due in 61 days. That's what you got… no more no less!"

"Michael, you don't have to worry. We don't have 61 days to make this happen. It must work as soon as possible."

Sir Arthur insisted that Aaron and Michael use his plane on the trip to Tel Aviv.

Michael called Doria.

"My love, I am still here with Sir Arthur and I will be extending my stay. How are you feeling?"

"Oh, I'm fine, I imagine there is a lot to cover. We are all fine here. Let me know your plans. I know you will call every day you can."

Michael always had that very special feeling when he landed in Israel. He remembered the first time he arrived. It was the land of milk and honey, and his mother reading to him stories in Arabic about his heritage and the land of his ancestors. It brought back memories of how his involvement occurred with the Mossad. In a sense it seemed like yesterday, and in another a million years ago.

The Mossad got started with his new identity and education. They didn't have to make him much older but he needed a beard, luckily that would happen quickly. He spoke both dialects fluently and been through the initiation course a number of times. He had been tutored in the nuances of an Arab man.

Jamil Abbas was coming to life. They fitted him with a new wardrobe as well as with passport, business and credit cards. He was a member of a Turkish bath and photos of his wife, children and mistress. He had business cards of companies in Europe and the Middle East. He had started to grow a beard before he left for Israel. All male Iraqis had beards of some kind. He had a crash course in munitions and weaponry. The boys had already drawn up a list of weapons and munitions. The discussion centered on how he possibly could be contacted through the French munition agents. It had to be a joint effort of using Sir Arthur and Michael.

CHAPTER

NINE

THE FRENCH CONTACT was Marcel Axcel who was the major resource for all types of weaponry and munitions. He had an international reputation and as most arms dealers centered his business in the Banana Republics, Africa, the Middle East, and South America.

Axcel industries was wired into the French munitions industry and found a way to "create" overruns of the key military items that were wanted by his clientele. Marcel was about sixty years old, tall extremely good looking with gray hair and beard. He only wore Armani suits and drank the best champagne. He was divorced with grown children and seemed to have a number of women attracted to him. Marcel found a way to eliminate his major competitors and solidify his position with the premier aircraft manufacturers. He lived on the Right Bank in the heart of the boutiques right off Rue St. Honore.

Aaron flew back to London to work with Sir Arthur on their strategy for reaching Marcel Axcel. It had to be flawless. Sir Arthur had an international reputation and the Mossad was certain Marcel would be flattered to receive a call from such a renowned person.

Sir Arthur's part would be to put Marcel together with Mr. Abbas and nothing else. The Mossad did not want to involve him any more than referring him to Michael. The Mossad's agents in Paris had spent time not only learning about Marcel's operation, but his lifestyle and what, if necessary, it would take to make him cooperate. That would be the last resort. The plan was based on Michael being in Iraq when Marcel Axcel needed to reach him. That was the part of the plan that no one could pin down. There had to be a meeting with Sir Arthur and Marcel for anything to happen.

Michael's program was complete; he had three days to learn the munitions business. Naturally his education centered around the list of armaments needed. He was torn between helping Israel and home with Doria. He had been to Baghdad before when he and Bengy wanted to take down Herr Schmidt who had the plans for the V2 rocket. Michael made it a priority to walk the city and to know all means if necessary to escape his enemy.

He was met by an Iraqi professor of history who was a Sayan, a helper of Israel. Michael was taken to an apartment building where he met his so-called wife. The children were away visiting. There wasn't any question that his identity would be checked. The next day he went to the office in the center of the city. The Mossad had staff there to continue the charade. The company name was International Products. He now had to wait for Sir Arthur to make the connection with Marcel and then with himself. The check out process would now begin.

Sir Arthur was ready and a call was placed to Axcel International.

The receptionist put the call through to Marcel,

"Good morning, Sir Arthur."

"I only know you from reputation as being the premier retailer in this world. I am honored to receive this call."

"I wouldn't call me the premier retailer. But just a observant merchant who knows his way around."

Marcel laughed.

"I bet… Tell me to what do I owe this call. I'm extremely curious."

Sir Arthur spoke French fluently so the conversation was moving along. Marcel loved fashion and was asking all types of questions about the industry. It created a great atmosphere for what Sir Arthur wanted to say.

"I have an interesting proposition for you. It involves my participation and my associate. I prefer not to discuss the topic over the phone. I would like to set up a meeting either in Paris or here in London. Naturally, if you come here, I will show you throughout our facilities, which are state of the art."

"Sir Arthur I have not been to London for quite some time and I would love to come and discuss this proposition. Your invitation to see your operation is one I could not refuse.

When are you free?"

"How about next week, this week is gone, let's do it Tuesday. I can send my plane if you wish."

"That won't be necessary. I have one of my own."

Before Michael left Israel, he placed a call to Doria.

"My love, I am about to leave Israel and go to Iraq. I did not tell to you about this when we spoke last. I apologize for not coming forth with this necessary venture. Israel needs me to set up a program that will give them the opportunity to purchase the weapon systems they desperately need. I shall not be in any danger. It's basically an administrative operation. I will be in Iraq for a short time."

"I will telex you every day from the office; I do not want you to answer unless the baby is coming early. I will be fine and hopefully Israel will be able to get what they need. Sir Arthur is involved and we both have signed off on this project. I love you. Please tell Abe and Sarah."

"Michael, I love you. I understand, take care."

She hung up the phone, and thought how she had lived through this crisis before. She had faith in him and believed he was doing what needed to be done.

Michael received word that Sir Arthur had done his part and a meeting was scheduled. He expected that Marcel would be checking on his associate shortly.

Michael spent his time learning about Baghdad. He decided to go back to the Basra Road and the square where the Kurdish Rebels known as the Peshmerga massacred close to eighty people. It included Herr Schmidt who had the plans for the V2 rockets. They were part of the KDP, The Kurdish Democratic Party. The horrors of that evening returned. He needed to wait and waiting was not easy for Michael.

Marcel Axcel arrived on his jet in style and was met by Sir Arthur's new Bentley. When the pleasantries were over, they were served coffee and scones.

Marcel remarked,

"Sir Arthur, the view from your office is spectacular and our little chat has been quite informative. My curiosity is just about at its highest point. Why am I here?"

"Marcel, you don't mind me calling you Marcel."

"No, not at all."

"I have a number of investments in other businesses around the world. They are quite different from the apparel and retail industry. They range from enterprises that are quite above board and some are just on the line. I believe I do not have to draw you a picture of what on the line means."

"I am aware of what you are saying. It seems we both play in an area that is quite not totally legal."

"Marcel, I am associated with a group in the Middle East headed by my associate who is acquiring products that you are able to deliver. I would like you to contact this person and see if you can become a resource for his needs. If this is of interest to you, I will supply the necessary information so that a program can be worked out. I know it can be a very profitable venture."

"Naturally I did not expect this type of conversation. However, I am interested in doing business with you. I like the relationship and if we can work out a program, I am interested."

"Let's have lunch and I will show you through the facility"

Not only did he show Marcel the operation but he took him to the design/product development center.

"Marcel, as you know we have a group of better men's stores called Savior Faire. The materials we use are in the Armani category mainly from Zegna, in Northern Italy. They are some of the finest fabrications in the world.

Let's make you a suit of your choice… here are the latest materials."

Marcel's measurements were taken and as Sir Arthur stated, the suit would be made in the sample room in an hour or sec.

He could not believe it could be done. They sat down on the sofa in Sir Arthur's office

"What I would like you to do is contact my associate who is in Iraq. I've written down all the necessary information on how he can be reached. He will have a shopping list of his needs. I would hope that we could bring this venture to fruition and build an ongoing relation together. My associate has my complete confidence, backing, and speaks for me."

"Sir Arthur, I would like this relationship to work. I like your world and want to know more about it. I will contact this person quickly and see what we can do together, I came here not knowing what to expect. Let's see if the cooperation between us can work."

His secretary came in the office with a large box.

"Sir Arthur, here is the suit that you ordered."

Marcel was amazed.

"I hope you can react to this project as quickly as the suit was made, wear it well."

They both laughed.

"If you need anything or additional information here is my private member. Call me anytime."

Marcel was impressed and when he arrived in Paris, he immediately contacted his people in Iraq. He wanted them to check this person out and to have the associate contact him directly.

Michael received a message from Aaron that the meeting with Marcel Axcel went well and to expect an inquiry shortly. It didn't take long that Mr. Arif appeared at his office requesting to see Mr. Jamil Abbas. He showed his business card representing Axcel International.

"I am here at the request of Mr. Marcel Axcel to make an appointment for him to speak to you directly. We are interested in knowing more about your business dealings here."

"I am in the import/export business handling all types of merchandise that can generate sales. As you, that business is difficult to display and to pinpoint. It includes many areas where a blind eye to the law as necessary. My needs at the moment can best be served with what Axcel International can supply. I believe we understand one another."

Mr. Arif has done his homework before the meeting. The work done by the Mossad to create a cover for Michael worked perfectly.

Mr. Arif continued,

"Mr. Axcel will call you and set up a meeting. He wants to see you and go over your possible purchases from our stock."

Michael had the secretary bring in coffee with some sweets and they continued the conversation.

"I will await his call."

Mr. Arif gave him a contact number for Axcel international if he didn't hear from Mr. Axcel in two days.

"I will try to have Mr. Axcel reach you within that period. We will see each other again if there is a business relationship."

Michael telexed the boys after the meeting. The call from Marcel Axcel came much quicker than expected.

"Mr. Abbas, I suppose you speak English which is the way I would like to communicate. I had a very good meeting with your associate Sir Arthur and would like to see if we can do business. This cannot be done over the phone. It demands a meeting face to face. I am not scheduled or about to come to Iraq, I suggest we meet here in Paris or another major city in Europe. I believe you and Sir Arthur wish to move quickly. If there is a reason to do business, I am open this next two weeks for a meeting. You have my telex number; naturally I prefer Paris or Italy. Let me know."

They spoke about Sir Arthur and how much he enjoyed visiting Fantastique. He seemed wanting to do business if it worked.

Michael reached Aaron and Joshua and reiterated the conversation with Marcel.

"The question is should we meet in Paris or is it better in Italy? I can tell him I only can get a visa for Italy if necessary. It seems he's more than willing to meet there. I leave the decision to you. It doesn't make any difference to me."

"We think we prefer Italy to get him to move off his home turf. We want to be on equal footing and setup the meeting for early next week. You would fly to Rome and workout the list of what we need. We will need the time together explaining some of the weapon systems and naturally tricking."

"If it's Italy then Rome or Milan are the obvious choices. However, let it be his choice."

Michael arrived.

"I want you to call Doria and tell her I'm fine and will call her from Europe when I arrive."

Michael sent the following telex,

"Dear Mr. Axcel

I would like us to meet in Italy, the choice of locations there is yours. I have a visa for Italy and it is more convenient. I have a working knowledge of the language. If this works for you, we should meet in six days. Please advise full detail."

Marcel answered quickly,

"Italy is fine. I have a villa in Florence and it will be an opportunity to visit and do our business. You will receive a telex within the hour with my contact information. We will meet 6 days from today on the fifteen on the 15th of the month at 10 AM."

Marcel liked the idea; he hadn't been to Florence in six months and he could make arrangements easily.

Michael was actually surprised when he saw the telex.

"Florence, I didn't expect that. It brings back a lot of memories. Good and bad."

He thought of his confrontation with Hans Streger.

He decided that he would move out of the apartment and find a hotel. He felt insecure and vulnerable in those surroundings. If anything went wrong, he did not want to involve the professor or his supposed family.

CHAPTER

TEN

IRAQ WAS ONE of the countries to which Nazis and the war criminals of the third Reich fled. They were helped by an organization of the Nazi elite called the Odessa. The name was used to identify the member of the SS that planned the escapes. It was setup in 1944 and helped their comrades to flee Europe mainly to the Middle East and South America.

When Schmidt left Germany after trying to kill Michael and his family, he went to Iraq and became part of the Nazi community.

Bengy Barak from the Mossad, who spoke perfect German was used as a means to reach Schmidt and spent time with the Nazi. Michael was part of the plan to retrieve the V2 rocket plans from Schmidt and was well known by his association with Schmidt and the Nazi community.

Mr. Arif, the representative for Axcel International, was also associated with other munitions dealers and a group of Neo-Nazis who were interested in any transaction that included contraband.

When Arif told his Nazi friends about a pending deal with Mr. Abbas, they wanted to know who this person was. They brought up his name at their weekly meeting and sent their members out to find out all they could about him.

They did their homework far better than Mr. Arif. They realized Mr. Abbas was not who he said he was. They looked at the photos they had of Michael, Schmidt, and Bengy and came to the conclusion that he was an Israeli spy and possibly buying weapons for Israel.

Mr. Arif was not informed.

The Nazis wanted to "speak" to Mr. Abbas and question him on his relationship with Schmidt. They were more than interested in his activities in Iraq.

The question before the group was after interrogation should he be eliminated? They had already marked him as a Zionist spy.

Michael wanted to leave as quickly as possible. Michael had booked his flight to Rome and proceeded to make reservations to drive to Florence. There was not daily service to Rome. He booked the next available flight which was in two days.

He decided to stay at the Hotel Rashid in downtown Baghdad. He chose this hotel because it catered to international business men. Baghdad was now a city of close to a million people and in the 1970's prospering.

Baghdad was born in 762 and was part of the Abbasid Dynasty of Caliphs for 500 years. During this time, it was the center of Arab and Islamic civilization; Baghdad was considered the greatest city of its time. The Mongols conquered it in 1258 and the city ceased to be a beacon in the Arab world.

It did not take long for the Neo-Nazis to find where Michael was staying. They had the information from Mr. Arif, where he had his office and followed him to his hotel. They decided to kidnap and interrogate him. The group had their members to continue to follow him wanting to find out if he had comrades or other business.

Michael had been trained by the Mossad to detect anyone who was interested in his movements.

He spotted those following him almost immediately and needed a plan to lose them. Michael became deeply concerned when he realized he was being followed by more than one group… possibly two different groups.

The time he spent walking the city was about to pay dividends. He took them away from the Hotel Rashid and on to Palestine Street and Al-Khulafa Streets by the great mosque in to the vast market places of the Baghdad bazaars.

He had a Mossad contact in Baghdad and needed to reach him. Whoever was following him knew of his hotel and would have someone there to see his return. His "excursion" through the teaming market places eliminated at least one group that was following. He was not sure about the other.

He continued his adventure through the markets. The throngs of people buying every conceivable item was the perfect cover to lose his pursuers. He wondered who they were and why they were looking for him. Somehow, they knew he was there. Did they know the reason why? He did not want to stop and call until he felt they were gone. Finally, he felt he had "lost" them and dialed his contact.

"I would like you to meet me and I will give you the key to my hotel room and retrieve my belongings. I have the address of the emergency safe house and will be able to make it there. It should not be an issue. The hotel lobby is always busy. You should be able to enter without being noticed I will continue my walk and will show up at the house at dark. I will not come until I know I have lost them."

He could only think of certain people who would want him in their grasps.

1. The police… highly unlikely
2. The munitions people for further questioning… really not an option.
3. Something from the past… Egyptians or Nazi enemies.

It was one or the other—the latter more of a possibility

After passing the key he went off in a different direction and realized he was still being followed…

He did not believe they saw him pass the key to the Mossad agent.

His best bet was the market places. They went on for literally miles and at this time of day a mass of shoppers. They were still two of them, and they did not give up even though they lost him for over an hour. Michael was mad at himself for he forgot the cardinal rule; don't underestimate your opponent. Somehow, he came to the conclusion there was now only one tracker. The other either gave up or went off in a different direction. Michael had his gun with him and felt he could elude his pursuers and get the flight to Rome.

He had another identity with him which would make him difficult to track. When he was sure that it was one assailment tracking him, he could possibly go on the offensive. He soon realized he was right and maneuvered himself behind the pursuer. He might be able to get some answers if the situation arose that he corners him and "asked" a few questions. He followed him for a while; the man seemed to be still looking for him. All his actions were along those lines. They approached a narrower part of the bazaar with many uninhabited alleys. Michael made his move and shoved his gun in to the back of the Neo-Nazi.

"Who are you and why are you following me?" Steinberger was stunned and blurred out in broken English… nothing, and then in German "nicht".

He was not about to say anything and Michael realized he made a mistake. Michael pushed him up the wall.

"You have been following me why?"

Steinberger said nothing; just stared at Michael and then spit in his face.

"Juden! (Jew)"

He pushed Michael away and pulled a Luger pistol from his pocket. Michael shot him in the head and he died instantly.

He slowly lowered his body to the ground, retrieved his wallet and wristwatch and whatever he had in his pockets. No one heard the shot; the noise level in the market was always at the highest decimal. The alley was empty. Michael laid him down as if he was sleeping and walked away. Michael was in shock. He had fired at the enemy but never killed a man at this close range. He made his way to the safe house. It took him over an hour for he wanted to make sure he wasn't followed.

How did I get myself into this? Why did I pull the trigger? Was it necessary to kill him? What could I have done differently? The questions kept coming up as he sought the refuge of the safe house. He finally reached his destination and the Mossad agent was there with his bag. Dov, the Mossad agent, gave him a rundown.

"I did not have any problems at the hotel. I cleaned out the room and wiped it down so there aren't any finger prints."

"They have my credit card on file so they will automatically bill the card."

Michael relayed the story to Dov.

"What you did you had to do," Dov understood how he felt. "You used your head and made it difficult for the police to identify him. He was a Nazi that you can be sure of. We will get you out of Iraq as planned. You have the additional identity which you will use. Life goes on."

Michael looked at him.

"I wish I could chalk it up to experience; it will be with me forever."

As soon as he touched down in Rome, he called Doria. They talked for twenty minutes and off he went to meet Aaron and Joshua. All three drove to Florence. The boys had not seen Michael for almost ten days and he looked very Iraqi with his dark complexion and full-grown beard.

Michael relayed the story of Iraq omitting the killing incident; they had three days for the meeting to bring Michael up to speed on weapons and munitions.

They stayed on the outskirts of Florence at the Villa Cora hotel off Viale Michelangelo. It was the same area where they had a firefight with Streiger and company. Aaron and Joshua brought different passports for Michael and themselves if needed.

Marcel Axcel had a villa in a beautiful section of the city, called Bellos Guardo, which translated as beautiful view. When you see most of the art books on Florence, they picture the dome of the Duomo on the cover. That photo was taken from Bellos Guardo.

Aaron and Joshua scouted the property around Axcel's villa. They wanted to know the terrain just in case. They got down to discussing how Michael would present his list of weapons and structure the payments.

They came up with a list of weapons that were centered around the Mirage III. It was the plane that was so successful demolishing the Egyptian and Syrian air force in the Six Day War. It was a proven in combat for its low-cost maintenance. The actual costs were lower in relation to what it delivered. Israel needed as many aircraft as possible and their spare parts. France produced these fighters for export. The question was it possible to become the buyer of orders destined for Argentina, Pakistan, and Libya?

Aaron and Joshua had acquired the number of aircraft that were available through their sources. They had the combined numbers of aircraft on order of their foes. It did not include what Axcel International had in their hands.

The negotiation was the key, what the actual position and power that Axcel had was a question mark in regards to the Mirage. Did he have a significant amount of air craft available for sale?

Michael had a list of the weaponry

Anti-tank weapons.

Missiles for the Mirage

Attack helicopters

Armed personnel carriers

These were the main items beside the Mirage.

Michael went over the list.

"Guys, this is going to be a hard sell. Taking goods from some of his customers to sell to us is a tall order. I imagine we are more than willing to pay top dollar. We'd better be or we won't be in the ball game."

"The French have an embargo on those nations directly involved in the '67 war. They are selling weapons to Libya and Iraq who were not involved. This could be our opening.

They discussed the strategy for a day and a half and realized there were pieces they could not control; the negotiation was everything.

Marcel arrived in his jet with a very sheek lady on his arm and two bodyguards. There was a car waiting and they made their way to Bellos Guardo. Michael took the rental car to the meeting and arrived right on schedule. The Villa was situated on the top at the top of the hill in a grove of eucalyptus trees and a well-designed garden surrounding the villa. It was probably more than one hundred fifty years old. Inside it was about as contemporary as could be and furnished with impeccable taste.

Marcel greeted him warmly.

"Mr. Abbas, it is a pleasure to meet you. Thank you for coming to Europe. Have you been to Florence before?"

"Yes, I have done considerable business in Italy and Florence is my favorite city."

"Well… I see we have a lot in common, because it's also mine. As I said when we spoke, I'm fond of your associate Sir Arthur. I enjoyed meeting him and seeing the operation. In fact, he made me a fashion suit in two hours. It was almost unbelievable."

They both laughed.

"How long have you been associated with Sir Arthur?"

"I went to work for Fantastique in my teens and was fortunate to be in the right place at the right time. Sir Arthur liked my work and acted as my protégé. He sent me to Harvard and to their business school which resulted in me being able to earn a major position in his organization. Inow have an American accent when I speak English."

They both laughed.

Michael continued, "My family was originally from the Middle East and I speak a number of Arab dialects."

They wandered out on the terrace. One of the bodyguards brought cappuccino and Italian pastry to the patio table.

"I think we should talk here. Let's take advantage of this beautiful day," said Marcel.

While Michael was giving Marcel his resume, his sixth sense was working. He had the distinct feeling that Marcel was not only a notorious munitions dealer, but somehow had a bond with Michael's heritage.

Michael didn't want to originate the main topic. He wanted Marcel to bring it up. He continued talking about his role and Sir Arthur in their varied business ventures.

Marcel spoke first on the subject matter.

"I guess the small talk is over and we should discuss what you came for. I presume it's a shopping list of merchandise that I have available or can obtain."

"You are correct, we are looking for a number of different weapon systems that you can procure for clients, mainly in the Middle East. I would prefer not to mention the name if that is possible."

"I didn't expect anything different. Actually, I do not wish to know the final destinations. I am not bound by any allegiance to any group or entity. I believe we understand one another. So, what does this list include?"

"Mainly advanced weaponry:

Mirage III and spare parts

Missiles for the fighters

Anti-tank weapons

Armored personnel carriers

Grenade launchers.

Michael continued.

"The key item is the Mirage and its spare parts. The rest of the shopping list we can live without if necessary. That's it, no stories, straight to the heart of the matter."

"Why do you think I can deliver Mirages?"

"We know you have them and are able to have them rerouted from other customers to us. We realize this is not an easy task but we believe if you wish to do it, it will happen."

Marcel smiled.

"You are quite the associate. I believe you are more than a deliverer of messages."

"I believe we understand one another and can make this work."

"What are you prepared to offer to create an incentive for my organization to reconsider the rerouting of the merchandise?"

"The going price plus a bonus that is fair and equitable."

"And what if I say no…"

"Sir Arthur and I will find a way for you to reconsider."

"Interesting, I thought you might say that."

Michael replied,

"We feel selling to the Libyan and Iraqi regime and others is not good politics and not in your best interest. You would be alienating the United States and Britain and others. You would be helping people who aren't interested in you and your operation. In plain English… you don't fuck with the powers to be… or Mother Nature. I believe we both understand one another."

Marcel continued.

"You have laid out an interesting proposition. For argument sakes, how many Mirages are you willing to take?"

"In so many words, all that you have available. Which means those planes destined for Libya and Iraq. I believe it's 50 plus aircraft. We need at least 30–35 and are greedy and want them all."

Michael continued.

"I have people here that can work out the details with on the entire shopping list and the pricing. They are part of our organization."

Marcel walked to the edge of the patio.

"I wouldn't have thought differently," he said as he smiled.

"I have some additional questions, for example, where are the Mirages?"

"They are in the south of France. Most of it ready to be loaded on freighters and super cargo vessels in the next weeks. The additional spare parts are not far behind. We have the means to move the merchandise.

"Mr. Abbas, if that is your real name, I am impressed with your style. I realize who I am dealing with and respect what you are doing. My major function is to move merchandise at the most favorable prices. I believe we can come to an agreement as you outlined. Send your people over later today and we will work out the details. You and I will have dinner and I will wear my Sir Arthur's suit."

Aaron and Joshua met with Marcel in the afternoon and the following morning. They arrived at pricing and went over the delivery issues. There would be additional meetings more likely in Paris or the port of Marseille.

They went over the additional equipment they had on their list and worked out a delivery schedule.

It took them a good portion of the day. Michael showed up when they were still working out the details. He wanted to speak to Marcel.

The question was how they could move the equipment as quickly as possible. That point he had to leave to Joshua and Aaron. Time was of the essence.

Marcel looked up and saw Michael.

"Well, if it isn't Mr. Abbas. I enjoyed dinner last evening and Anna thought you were exciting."

They laughed.

"I hope we can become good friends and spend time together. I know Sir Arthur and I would love to see you in London. You might even end up with another suit!!"

Michael could not wait to call Sir Arthur with the news. He was elated and told Michael to sit still. He was sending his plane to take him to Boston.

He called Doria who was overjoyed.

Michael slept most of the way home dreaming his reoccurring nightmare. There was an addition, Mirages flying in formation overhead.

CHAPTER
ELEVEN

THE WAR OF Attrition went on not just in Israel. A group attached to the PLO high jacked four planes and landed three in Jordan near Amman. After the foreign national hostages were taken off the planes, three of the planes were blown up in front of the international press. There was pressure from the Arab governments condemning the hijacking. Arafat's famous quote was born, "Our basic aim is to liberate the land from the Mediterranean Sea to the Jordan River! Thus, the slogan "from the river to the sea". The suicide bombings, the targeting of Israeli citizens increased dramatically. Michael heard Greta's story about what happened in Germany when he arrived. She was still visibly shaken with the ongoing vendetta against her.

Experiencing Heinz Adler's attack with a knife was not going to go away. She would need time to regain her composure and come to grips with the incident. She was well aware of Michael being attacked at his office by the Neo Nazis. Could this happen to me was pressing or her psyche. Michael arranged for a security person to accompany her everywhere she went. It made her slightly more comfortable. She was always on guard and carried the Glock pistol wherever she went. Her episode awakened Michael that another attempt on his life and family was more than a possibility. He doubled the security details around Doria and the company in general.

Michael had not spent time with Abe or Sarah. He needed to catch up on the legal and financial doings while he was away; they met over dinner.

Abe continued the conversation.

"Michael, I do not see any major issues that could arise as of this moment. Sir Arthur's organization has been extremely cooperative. Our lawyers and financial people seem to be working extremely well with their organization. I know that Arthur has given them marching orders to get this done and without delay. Any points of disagreements have been cleared up almost immediately. I know it's Arthur's doing.

"For your information all the real estate that Fantastique owns is part of the sale. We will own at least 50 to 60 major pieces of property. It could be as many as 100. It's hard to believe."

Michael thought about the news. He was amazed.

Michael continued his thoughts to Abe and Sarah.

"The fusion of the two organizations cannot happen overnight. It will take a period of time and going through the learning curve to achieve what we are after. Sir Arthur has made it a lot easier. His organization knows his wishes and is performing as he outlined. Our job is to make sure we create a culture that does not put one organization against the other."

Michael's attention was now with Doria, the coming addition and his family. He felt he had let them all down with the course of events that forced him to the service of Israel. He was torn between the two and tried to keep all the balls in the air. He had not spent time with his mother Hannah and sister Rachel which was out of character. The course of events had made it very difficult and he wanted to make amends.

He spoke to Sir Arthur daily, actually more than once. Their ability to communicate on all levels made the impeding new corporation move along at a rapid pace.

"Arthur, as you know I have had a very little experience in menswear. You have a group of twenty stores called Savoir Faire that look great. I am a novice here and need help."

"Michael, you need not worry; you will learn this area of the business quickly. I also have a superb person who runs the stores and the buying. By the way… You dress just like the store's image. You have a lot more to worry about."

While the new owner of Fantastique was busy working in London, there were forces in Germany that were interested in his demise. Both he and Greta were in their crosshairs. Herr Rudolph Gruder was an influential member of the Aryan National Party. He had managed to avoid the Allied War Commission on war criminals by getting papers off a dead comrade. He had made arrangements to find Greta and discover what transpired in the Adler/Schneider deaths. He wanted to know the particulars of why the V2 rocket program failed. There wasn't a clear picture of what actually happened. The bodies of both men and the additional casualties of the group were found at their headquarters. All Gruder knew was that some sort of agreement had gone astray in paying the ransom for Greta Hirsh.

There had to be other reasons. They learned from Schneider about plans for the V2 rockets that were not destroyed and both Adler and Schneider were trying to acquire them. Greta Hirsh had knowledge of their location. The entire story had to be verified by Greta. She also needed to be eliminated as a traitor to the Reich. When the plan fell apart, he was upset with the miscues by his group. He felt better when he was given her personal information. The real estate forms for selling her condominium revealed her U.S. location. Gruder was able to make the connection between Greta and Michael. He had done his research and came to the conclusion they had been in this charade together. He assumed there was a connection in a clandestine operation. When the news of Michael and Fantastique broke, Gruder thought he had the opportunity to eliminate an adversary.

Most of the terrorist groups of the world maintain connections with each other. Information was passed around that would help organizations acquire their needs from weaponry, drugs, to information. Gruder wanted to reach the leadership of the IRA, principally the provisional IRA. This group was committed to wage an "armed struggle" against British Rule in Northern Ireland. He was willing to pay handsomely for the organization to kill Michael.

What the Aryan Party did not know was that the IRA botched the kidnapping of Edward Heath, the Prime Minister because of Michael's actions. When Gruder made the request, he got an immediate reply for they also wanted retribution. "It will be done."

The provisional IRA was not only interested in Michael but also in Sir Arthur since his retail outlets in Northern Ireland were Pro-Heath or should we say Pro-Protestant in their minds. The IRA wanted to devise a plan that would possibly take out both at the same time. They requested any information the Aryan Party had on Michael Jannsen. They were not interested in his connection to Israel; he had foiled their attempt on Edward Heath. He was now allied with Sir Arthur who was in their estimation anti-Catholic.

They went about doing their surveillance which included knowing the schedule of both. They wanted to find them together. They realized this plan would take time since Michael did not have a definitive schedule in the U.K. He came when needed at the spur of the moment. Sir Arthur was predictable for the most part. He was in the office approximately the same times daily. His schedule was very consistent.

The baby was four to eight weeks away and Michael really didn't want to go anywhere. Doria was, as the saying goes, "big as a house". She looked like she could deliver anytime or maybe it was twins. There was plenty to do in Boston and he could confer with Sir Arthur easily for there was a five hour difference in time. He was going to stay close to home unless there was a disaster.

Aaron and Joshua wanted to follow up with Michael and fill him in on the final elements of acquiring the Mirages and the balance of the shopping list. They were in awe how Michael had made the deal. He had made his strategy based on what he saw in Marcel Axcel's character. He got the immediate impression that somewhere in this man's head was something that made them bond.

Marcel asked Michael,

"What if I had said no and meant it?"

"We would have had to kill you… will you pass the rolls."

Anna, his girlfriend, almost fell off her chair.

CHAPTER

TWELVE

MICHAEL HAD ODD feeling for Marcel and felt he was going to have a new friendship. It was his sixth sense sending him a message.

It started off as a strange conversation before they actually discussed the deal. Michael immediately took a liking toward him and wanted to know more about him. He started the conversation.

"Marcel, you seem to be a duck out of water as we say in America."

"What do you mean?"

"Well, you're in a profession that doesn't fit your character and personality. I would have thought you would be in some sort of public relations, retail or the fashion business, or the arts."

"It's funny you say that because as a university student I wanted to be involved in the arts and the fashion industry. I actually took classes in design.

"So, what happened?"

"I started working for these people who had a variety of interests, one of them being munitions and their sales worldwide. They liked me and gave me the opportunity to become an important part of their organization.

"I performed beyond their expectations. The rest is history."

"I thought somewhere in your past you had this creative streak or should I say desire. When Arthur told me how excited you were about the product development center at Fantastique, I thought these are not the average comments of a munitions dealer.

"Even in our limited conversation now, I had the feeling that the creative part of your life was looking for an outlet."

"You're probably right, my grandfather left Russia and brought the family to France after World War I; he was an artist."

Michael hesitated for a moment and continued the conversation.

"I guess we have more in common than I thought. You're quite different than I expected and I am pleasantly surprised. You live in a very different world than I do. It's kind of strange on the one hand, I detest what you do, and on the other I value your friendship."

"I can't blame you for feeling as you do. I plan to address some of these issues shortly."

Michael was concerned about Marcel and his decision to renege on the Mirage contracts with Iraq, Libya, and the others.

That was not only bad for Marcel's business; it created more than a possibility of retribution being on the table. Michael thought there was probably already partial payments made on the goods.

Marcel was not a neophyte; he had been dealing in this clandestine business for years. Axcel International had security in place to protect him and key personnel.

Michael continued the conversation.

"Marcel, I know we paid you well for the equipment. I also know that you have burned most of the bridges with many of your customers by working with us. On that alone we can never repay you.

"We have become friends and I know you would come to my aid if necessary. We, Bengy and the boys, want you to know that we are here to help in any way. We have your back!"

"I appreciate your concern and know exactly what I have done and the possible repercussions. I am just sixty years old and money is the least of my issues. I am planning in the near future of walking away from this business and becoming a competitor to you and Sir Arthur."

They started to laugh.

Marcel continued,

"Seriously I have been thinking of sailing off in the sunset for quite some time. I didn't expect to do it in this manner, but circumstances dictate events. What probably put me over the edge was something I haven't spoken about to anyone. My dad who died when I was 12 years old was Jewish."

"I'm not surprised after hearing your family history. Welcome back. Shalom."

"I want you to keep in touch and contact Bengy or Aaron and Joshua if there are any rumblings that could turn into threats."

"My plans to leave this industry are not idle talk."

"Well, if you ever do, come see me. You have all the skills for organization. Anyone that can manipulate the French Aviation Industry to sell you planes is my kind of guy."

Michael had a long discussion with Aaron and Joshua in regards to protecting Marcel. He felt the Arab League would seek their pound of flesh over his Mirage sales to the Israelis.

He spoke to Aaron and Joshua.

"Guys, there isn't any question that Marcel is about to face some serious threats from his pissed off clientele.

"He has not only gone back on the deal but sold the products to their enemy.

"I can almost guarantee the news will be out overnight. Those planes were supposed to be on their way now and the customers will be aware of what happened within a day or two. We as well as Marcel can expect some sort of trouble."

Aaron interrupted Michael.

"Michael, we are well aware of what his actions will produce. The French will be on the war path and could create an international uproar as they did with the Cherbourg incident. If you remember, we stole boats and now planes. It could be a mess."

"We know there are government individuals that are involved in any of these ventures. There are payoffs and all types of mischief that goes on in anything to do with military equipment and government connections.

"As far as Marcel is concerned, we have already discussed this issue among ourselves. He will be covered by our two agents in Paris as best we can. He has security; we do not know to what extent we are expecting trouble.

I would venture to say the parties involved are already aware of the transaction."

Michael was in agreement, "I didn't think of that aspect. It stands to reason there are going to be some unhappy people from a monetary and political point of view.

"Marcel should take a vacation. It would be best staying in Florence and enjoy the view from his villa for at least a few weeks.

"I will speak to him and make him aware of what he already knows. There are other factors that are in play that need to be addressed."

Joshua had a few words to add. "We never really discussed the situation that developed in Baghdad. We should really address it."

Michael replied, "It is not open for discussion at this time. I will bring it up later. I am trying to live with the results. It is on my mind daily."

Marcel took the advice of Aaron and Joshua and decided to spend some time in Florence. He actually could conduct his business from his villa in Bellos Guardo.

He had all the necessary communication equipment, telex included, to function. He was concerned with his safety and telexed Paris to send an additional security person to Italy.

Anna was still there enjoying shopping on the Via Tornabuoni, the home of all the couture brands. She didn't miss the Ponte Vecchio where the windows were filled with the most exquisite jewelry.

Marcel, at this time, did not venture into the city, but stayed at the villa and enjoyed the patio along with the fantastic views of Florence and Tuscany.

He conducted his business and at the same time started to make plans for his future. His home was Paris, but he felt he needed to make a major change in his life. He wanted to consult with Michael about possibly coming to the United States. It could be Boston, or somewhere in New England.

He was in a business that you couldn't sell and it was not so simple to close it down. Real thought and planning were necessary to achieve that end and an answer. He now had the time to devote to that project. There were numerous conversations with Michael. He studied possible opportunities for a business venture in a number of locations. For the time being, he felt fairly secure here in Florence. While he contemplated his future, others were planning his demise.

At the Iraqi government meetings in Baghdad, the subject for discussion was the inability to procure the Mirage jets though they had placed the order with Axcel International. The merchandise was supposed to be shipped these past weeks. They received a telex from Axcel International stating that the merchandise was unavailable at this time. The delivery dates were pushed back over a year.

When the Iraqis questioned the new dates, they wanted to know why there was a delay and why were they not notified sooner. The answers were not forthcoming. Within days after receiving the answer, the Iraqis learned why there was a cancellation. They did receive their deposit and a letter of apology which only fanned the flames. The news in the Arab world travels quickly.

The decision was made to make Axcel International an example and to eliminate Mr. Axcel. The Falcon Intelligence cell of Iraq (FIC) was the organization that was given the Axcel project. The cancelation of the purchase was considered a crime against the state.

The FIC dispatched two agents to Paris. It did not take long to find out where Marcel was located. When they arrived in Florence, they went to the Iraqi Trade Office which was in an apartment building near the Stazione Centrale. They found a hotel in the vicinity of the trade office and started to make their plan. They did not speak Italian and their English was limited. Because they did not know the city, they needed help from the Iraqi staff in the trade office locating Mr. Axcel. They had acquired his Florence address from the Paris office.

They needed a car and used one of the Iraqi staff to make the arrangements. The two had never been to Italy; in fact, they had only traveled in the Middle East.

Florence, although a small city, was very complicated to navigate with an automobile. There was the Blue Zone where cars were not allowed. There were one-way streets everywhere. They needed time to learn the city and the area where Marcel lived.

Mr. Amal and Mr. Saif spent two days scouting the area around Belos Guardo and tried to get close to the villa without being noticed. They realized that Mr. Axcel had 24-hour security and that he seldom left the premises. They needed some type of diversion to eliminate or distract the security guards and possibly have him leave the villa. Mr. Saif came up with a plan to use some type of smoke bomb. They called the Iraqi embassy in Rome to obtain the articles needed. The embassy not only found what they requested but sent an additional person for the attack.

Marcel was starting to get cabin fever. He hadn't left the grounds since he arrived and wanted to go to the center. He wanted to shop for the latest fashion in men's sportswear. Marcel spent two hours shopping in the boutiques on Via Del Parione and wandered the area around Sante Croce and the Mercato San Lorenzo. He had his three bodyguards always with him. He was fluent in Italian and decided to stop at Michael's favorite store, the Alessi boutique, which was on the way back to his car.

The Iraqis had one of the group watching the villa on a daily basis. They did not want to attempt an assault if he went into the city. They realized that an attack of this sort would lessen the possibility of escape. They did not speak the language and would be easily identifiable. They were going to stay with the original plan.

The Iraqis decided that they had everything in place and proceeded with the attack early the next morning when there was hardly any traffic in the area. All the weapons were equipped with silencers. One of the group was able to work his way around the back of this property and would throw the smoke bomb through the patio windows. This would create havoc and force the occupants to leave through the front entrance, where they would be met with gun fire.

Marcel was up early and drinking a cappuccino at the kitchen counter. Two of his guards were on duty; the third had the morning off. Anna was still in bed. She was not an early riser. In fact, you seldom saw her face until 11:00 am. The kitchen faced the back of the house with huge glass doors that led to the patio. The smoke bomb shattered the glass and landed four to five feet to the side of Marcel.

Marcel did not panic. In fact, he did just the opposite. He had been in the Special Forces of the French army (COS) and trained to react to all emergency situations. He reached into the kitchen cabinet and retrieved his 9-millimeter Beretta. He had at least four in the villa in different rooms just for this type of situation. The smoke was not intense. He believed the smoke bomb only produced half of the smoke it was designed to dispatch.

Marcel saw the Iraqi reaching the patio door and about to enter the kitchen. Marcel shot twice, hitting him in the chest and shoulder. The Iraqi was down but not necessarily dead. Marcel picked up the bomb and threw it out on the patio.

The two bodyguards were attacked at the front entrance. They were retreating as the two Iraqis opened fire with machine pistols. The guards were at a disadvantage having only side arms. Marcel, realizing what was happening, went out on the patio and started to work his way around to the front entrance. He wanted to outflank the Iraqis.

As Marcel maneuvered himself into position, a strong hand came from nowhere and stopped him in his tracks.

"Mr. Axcel, greetings from Aaron, Joshua, and Michael. We are from the Mossad and have been asked to keep a watch on you. Let us handle the situation from here, and we will out flank the Iraqis with silencers on our weapons."

Yakov and his associates proceeded to disable Mr. Amar and Mr. Saif. Within 15 minutes, the entire incident was over. The sounds of gunfire were minimal due to the location of Marcel's villa. The Mossad removed the body and the two wounded Iraqis. Marcel reentered the villa and saw Anna wandering in the kitchen.

"What was all that noise this morning?" she asked. "It woke me."

Marcel answered, "We had the gardeners here. You're right. They were very noisy."

Marcel went to the phone and placed a call to Michael. "You certainly are a good friend. How can I ever thank you?"

"If I knew you could take care of yourself, we would not have bothered."

"I guess my army training came in handy."

Michael said, "What do you plan to do now?"

"I have had time to think about leaving the profession. Actually, I've been making some definitive plans. You might even have me as a neighbor."

"You probably will bring down the property values," Michael said. "Keep me posted."

Marcel put a new clip in his Barretta and double checked where the additional guns were located. He was not pleased with his bodyguards' performance and would make some changes soon.

CHAPTER

THIRTEEN

AARON AND JOSHUA arrived at the Fantastique office and needed to speak with Michael.

Joshua said,

"Michael, things are heating up and we want to fill you in. The politics are getting fierce and Golda is playing 'hard ball.' If you have a few minutes, we will give you our opinions about what we think of the situation. I don't know how much you know about Golda Meir but here is a quick history of this remarkable woman and where we are now.

"In 1969, Prime Minister Levi Eshkol died suddenly leading to the appointment of Yigal Allon as interim prime minister. There was an election to replace him. Golda Meir was voted the new party leader and served as Prime Minister, at the age of 71.

"In her early years she was the Jewish observer from Palestine to a conference called by Franklin D. Roosevelt to discuss the question of Jewish refugees fleeing Nazi persecution. Thirty- two countries expressed sorrow for the plight of the European Jews but refused to admit refugees. Throughout World War II she served several roles in the Jewish agency which functioned as the government of British Palestine.

I believe in 1965 the 67-year-old Meir was diagnosed with lymphoma and retired as foreign minister but continued to serve in the Knesset. She started serving as prime minister in 1969. Golda had mixed feelings due to her health concerns, but eventually agreed. Golda has made all the major decisions in bringing Israel into a possible major conflict."

"Now we are dealing with a serious threat."

"The Syrian president Hafez al-Assad has initiated a massive military buildup with a plan to reconquer the Golan Heights. He also wants to establish Syria as the dominant military power among the Arab countries. King Hussein of Jordan seems to be reluctant to engage in a new war. We believe he fears the possibility of losing even more territory than the West bank. He is also upset with Sadat's promise to support the PLO. There are two wars going on, us verses The Arab coalition, the other being Arab versus Arab."

"We have been fortunate in the past. The distrust and rivalries between the Arab States and Radical Arab groups allowed us to defeat them. It's apparent these factors allowed us to contend with superior numbers and resources. We are now confronting a new threat from Fatah. They have established a new organization called Black September named after the fighting between Arafat and Jordan. It amounted to what we call a Jordanian Civil War."

"They are performing strikes not only against Israel, but also outside of the Middle East as we have just seen in Munich with our athletes.

Golda is outraged at the perceived lack of global action, cutting off Jews fleeing Germany by not being able to migrate anywhere. She is so pissed off and has ordered us, the Mossad, to hunt down and assassinate any suspected leaders and operatives. She had declared war on Black September and will not take prisoners."

Joshua went on to give Michael a detailed report on the progress of moving the weapons.

When Michael returned from London, he brought back the style books of Fantastique's line development for the coming season. He wanted to know as much about Fantastique's development and business as he knew about his own.

Michael pinned up the sketches and photos of the line development on his cork walls. When he built his office, he had all the walls done in cork, so that all the development was within his view. He spent the better part of the day going over the programs they developed.

He was more interested in learning about their business than criticizing the collection. He called in some of the retail staff to look at the direction they had taken.

Greta came over from the product center and viewed them with Michael.

"These guys are really good at what they do; we can learn from them.

"Michael, what the hell is going on? Are you selling the business to Fantastique?"

"No, Greta. We are buying them."

Greta could not believe what she was hearing.

"Greta—I do not want you to say anything about what I just told you, I will let you know when it's official."

Michael thought of his dad who had died when he was six weeks old as he tried to focus on the sketches on the wall.

What would he do in this situation? Where would I be today if he had lived? Would I be a completely different person?

All these thoughts swirled around as he continued his critique. It was 2:00 am when the cork walls were a blur and he was forced to stop.

C H A P T E R
FOURTEEN

HERR GRUDER WAS losing patience with the IRA. He expected them to react quickly to their requests. The Aryan National Party had lost two key members and three additional members all attributed to Michael, Greta and the Israelis. The loss was even more catastrophic, since their program to rebuild the V2 rockets was derailed.

Gruder spoke to the Aryan Board.

"Gentleman since the IRA is not interested in our project, I propose we implement our own program. I know all of you want to revenge the deaths of our comrades. Let us make the necessary plans to achieve that end."

Herr Steiner spoke.

"Have you a plan or framework for us to consider?"

"Herr Michael Jannsen and Madame Greta Hirsh are in the United States. Our comrade Schmidt tried to eliminate Jannsen and failed. I have worked out a rudimentary idea that needs to be worked on. Naturally, there are two options. We want to kill both of them. I feel the only time you are going to have that opportunity is in the States. There has to be an element of surprise, I think that will be difficult because they are now on guard. We have to attack when they are most vulnerable. It will take at least six to eight trained personnel to carry out the mission. I have already sent Hans Kleinerman to Boston to check on their movements, schedule, and their security systems."

"When he returns this week, we will finalize our plans and move forward. To the 4th Reich, Heil Hitler!"

Herr Kleinerman returned from Boston and gave his full report.

"Herr Jannsen and Madame Hirsch work in the same office complex. The Stone offices are located in sort of an office park on the outside of the city; I believe is called Allston. There are many offices in the vicinity. It is a multi-story building with many employees. They have an adjacent facility less than 50 meters from the main office. This is what I believe is their product development facility. They have about twenty-twenty five people working there. It does not look like a normal office. They seem to be working on samples, grading patterns and a design area. They work a different schedule."

Gruder interrupted.

"What do you mean by a different schedule?"

"They seem to work late hours on a regular basis. Sometimes they are there late into the night. Other times they are not there until noon. Madame Hirsh spends a great deal of her time there working with the design people. The building is all glass and when it is late at night you can see everything.

"Herr Jannsen is there on a regular basis. He arrives from the main office always accompanied by a security guard who waits for him to return. There are three security people on duty continuously. I believe there are over one hundred fifty employees in the main office. There are signs everywhere telling where you can park your car. You cannot leave a car in front of the building. His wife who is pregnant is in the office daily as well as the owners Herr Stone and his wife. Security is at maximum efficiency. All employees have company door pass cards and I.D.'s. I believe these are the major points. I have drawn a map of the facility and its grounds. I believe that should cover the major points."

"Herr Kleinerman your report will enable us to form a plan. Just an additional question regarding the security people."

"What do you wish to know?"

"Most security people are generally there just to pass the time and are not committed to their job. Are the persons there serious? What is your opinion. You have watched them for over a week."

"Herr Gruder, these are professional guards. I believe they are ex-military men who know how to handle a weapon and not afraid to use it."

"Thank You."

That evening at the council meeting Herr Gruder was ready with his plan.

"Gentlemen, based on Kleinerman's report we need to mount a formidable assault on Jannsen and Hirsh. We need to make our strike when they are together at their facility near the office. We will need a force of at least six men to ensure success."

"I believe we will have to find the right time to strike when they both are in their product department. This means possibly spending sometime there before the operation, by that I mean the following. We will need someone always watching the complexes and informing the group when it is time to attack."

"Herr Jannsen always has at least an armed guard with him at all times which we can address. We believe Herr Jannsen will be in the office since his wife could possibly deliver in the next weeks. I believe we can assume those points. The time is right. I do not believe we will find a better time to mount the operation."

All the flight arrangements were made and also the accommodations.

Their exit plans were by car. When the mission was accomplished, they planned to drive to N.Y. and fly to Austria, Germany and Switzerland two on each flight. Gruder was flying to Zurich to transact some banking business at the same time.

They would use walky-talkies to communicate with each other. There would be a spotter on duty for all the hours the offices were open. Gruder estimated once they knew both were on site it would take ten to fifteen minutes for them to arrive. The group didn't know how long it would take to find them both together at the product center. Based on what he knew, it might take a day or two of waiting.

The group arrived on separate flights within two hours of one another. They waited for Gruder's flight and went to the hotel after picking up their rental cars. They did not bring any weapons. Gruder used his connections in the States to secure the necessary firepower. The weapons were delivered and included Walther P38, Lugers P08 for each man. Also enclosed was Meta Sub-Machine Guns all German made. They had come through Canada and were brought across the border. Gruder wanted weapons that were familiar to the participants. They were ready and needed to inspect the area around the building and the best ways out of the city and the road to N.Y.

They all had sacks, the kind paper boys slung over their shoulders to hold their automatic weapons.

The weather was too warm to try to conceal them under a coat. Herr Gruder felt confident the attack would be successful.

When the spotter saw them walking to the product center, he immediately signaled Herr Gruder. He did not inform him that both Michael and Greta were accompanied by two security guards. This time the guards entered the center with them which was quite unusual.

They were not the regular security people but Mossad and FBI operatives. They quickly herded all the employees into the back of the facility. Michael and Greta were included.

The FBI operative spoke,

"I want all of you to get down on the floor behind these tables, chairs and remain quiet. I am with the FBI and we are here to prevent a terrorist attack on this facility. We have a team of agents around the structure that will confront anyone entering. We have everything under control."

Michael yelled out,

"How the hell did you know?"

"Let's discuss that later. Please follow the instructions. We do not want anyone hurt."

Gruder and company planned to kill or disarm the guards at the entrance, enter the center and kill Michael and Greta. When they arrived at the walkway to the entrance they had their weapons in full view.

The product center was landscaped with trees and bushes surrounding the structure. When the Germans arrived, there wasn't a guard at the entrance, Gruder sensed something was wrong as a battalion of FBI agents along with German and Mossad personnel descended on them. His men opened fire and in less than 30 seconds most were either dead or severely wounded. Herr Gruder was mortally wounded and would die hours later at the hospital.

Michael's thoughts were everywhere. He wanted answers and they had to wait. His staff was in shock as well as Greta. Why was this happening again? How can I escape this world of constant danger? What have I done to put all that I love and cherish in peril? He didn't believe what he was seeing as Bengy, the Mossad, and the FBI agents appeared.

"Michael, I know you are shaken and pissed off. Let me tell you what happened after the incident with Greta and her connections to the Aryan

National Party and Adler. We needed to find out if they were a continued threat and put them out of business."

"We were able to place a mole in their organization and learned of a plan to kill you and Greta. We worked with the German secret service and the FBI to inform them of what Gruder had in store. We were not only able to stop them here but hopefully destroy their organization in Germany."

"I would like Greta to hear the rest of the story for we owe her for giving us the information to eliminate the Aryan National Party. If you remember, she went back to work for Adler and their relationship after she knew of their Nazi leanings. She was instrumental in charming the key people of the party, to give her sensitive information that we were able, to use to eliminate the party organization. We are forever in her gratitude."

Greta felt a great weight had been lifted off her shoulders. She was crying tears of joy.

Bengy went home with Michael and the whole story was told to Doria who just sat there listening and absorbing every word. When he was finished Doria looked at both of them.

"Bengy, is this the end or are we still in peril?"

"Doria, I really think we have finally put an end to this endless nightmare. I believe we have eliminated all the elements left over from the V2 rocket episode and its repercussions."

"I hope you are right… our baby needs a world that he's about to enter that is at peace. We both have paid a high price to reach that goal. We need closure."

The FBI tried to keep the incident from being national news and evented a story of drug dealers clashing with one another. It only made local news.

CHAPTER

FIFTEEN

THEY ALL HAD dinner and enjoyed one-another. Doria was tired and went off to bed. Michael and Bengy sat in the living room talking about the possible conflict.

Bengy started the conversation,

"Michael, Sadat has made a final peace offer that includes our withdrawal from the Sinai Peninsula. He relayed this to Henry Kissinger, who was secretary of state, via Sadat's advisor. Kissinger told Golda who then rejected the peace proposal because of its conditions returning to the 1948 boundaries. She knows the rejection can only mean going to war with Egypt. The Soviets and the Americans are pursuing detente and do not want the Middle East destabilized. We believe they have no control over the Egyptians. As far as we are concerned, we are on our way to war. The Egyptian army conducted military exercises near the border. It is just a question of when."

Michael was on the phone early the next morning relaying the story to Sir Arthur who took it all in.

"Michael. I realize where you have been as you Americans say 'through the mill'. You have a whole new world to explore and build on. I know all the experiences you've had are about to make you a better human being and a shrewder entrepreneur. You are about to be given the best gift in the world, a child. I want you to know that I will do whatever I can in the time I have left. I just signed the final papers making you the sole owner of Fantastique Ltd.

"You owe me one dollar. Congratulations!"

Michael held the phone after the call was finished. Realty was setting in. He was now worth in excess of one billion dollars and the responsibility for 18,000 employees.

He sat at the kitchen table and tried to put everything into proper perspective.

"How the hell did this happen?"

"It seems as if I was living in a dream."

Doria came into the kitchen

"You must be a rich man. You're talking to yourself."

"You have no idea how true those words are."

He proceeded to tell her about the call.

They both went off to the office and expected a deluge of calls once the news got out. It would not take long for the news to spread like wild fire, now that the lawyers and financial groups were not bound to secrecy. Bengy was there. He had made plans to leave later in the day. He congratulated them both and said he planned to call Sir Arthur. He had told Michael he would keep him updated on the situation through reports and military communiqués.

Abe and Sarah were there and they went into Michael's office. He closed the door.

"Almost all the people I love dearest are in this room. All of you have given me everything I desire in this life. We are about to enter an entirely new and different world and I want you to know that whatever we do, we do together. It is my responsibility to lead but only to a point. As I said to Sir Arthur it was a family decision… It still is."

There were two weeks of craziness with the press and social media. Michael's picture was in every magazine and newspaper. It was impossible to avoid the press and the endless telephone calls; Sir Arthur faced the same. They both spoke constantly on the final pieces of the merger and the sale. The world tried to find out what were the financial aspects of the merger to no avail. Sir Arthur had a group of his key people fly into Boston and give Michael the necessary information on how Fantastique functions. They were there to have Michael bless the game plan for the coming season and beyond. After the work day was done, Michael would study every store in the Fantastique chain. He was given a dossier on each of the fifteen hundred stores. It was a mammoth task.

Michael wanted to work from Boston until the baby was born. If he needed to be anywhere, Sir Arthur's plane, which was now his, was available at Logan airport. The meetings with the Fantastique group were going well. They spoke the same fashion language which made the transition much easier. Abe and Sarah were part of the group as well as Doria who insisted on being there. When Michael arrived at his office the head of security was waiting for him.

"Mr. Jannsen, we received this courier large envelope very early this morning. I had it tested for possible foul play. It has not been opened. It is somewhat rigid. I believe these could be photographs or something along those lines. I would like to be here when we open it. There isn't any return address. There is only your name and address. I wanted to make sure it was harmless."

Michael looked over the envelope. It had not come from overseas, for there were no such markings. He presumed it was sent locally and opened the envelope.

There seemed to be photographs between the sheets that protected them and a letter which he opened.

"Mr. Jannsen, we want you to be aware that we have Sir Arthur Brooks in our midst. We were able to insist on him accompanying us to an undisclosed location. He will be held here there until the sum of fifty million pounds is paid. For your information, he has been with us since early yesterday afternoon. The photos enclosed show his presence. We are extremely well organized and expedited the photos to you in the United States so you could see them this morning. We realize this has been quite a shock. You will receive further instructions on the process for the payment. We are only interested in payment. He will be returned when all demands are met. I would not recommend contacting Scotland Yard."

Michael immediately dialed Sir Arthur's private number and as expected there wasn't an answer. He checked with his secretary and heard that she had not seen him since he left for lunch yesterday.

He then called Bengy who was in Tel Aviv and gave him all the particulars.

"I realize you guys have your hands full with what's going on with your neighbors but Arthur and I need your help. What can you do?"

"Let me get the boys together and see where we are. In the mean time we have agents in the U.K. I will find out if they heard of anything."

Michael wasn't sitting still; he placed a call to Marcel Axcel.

"Marcel, there is an extremely important situation that I would like to discuss with you. This is not in relation to our program. I will meet you wherever you wish Paris, London, or Boston. But I need to address this issue as soon as possible."

"Michael, I can hear the urgency in your voice. My schedule is clear at the moment. I haven't been to Boston. I will be there tomorrow morning."

"Marcel, it's better we meet in London."

He then gathered Doria, Abe, and Sarah and gave them the news.

"I want you to know that I will commit all our resources and time to bring Arthur home. The world will need to stop turning until we bring him back. I swear on my yet to be born child!"

The war reports and analysis Bengy had arranged started arriving on Michael's desk.

In June 1973 Brezhnev, leader of the Soviet Union met with Richard Nixon and proposed that Israel pull back to its 1967 border.

Brezhnev said if Israel did not, "We will have difficulty keeping the military situation from flaring up." He felt under these circumstances Sadat will go ahead with a plan for war.

CHAPTER

SIXTEEN

Conrad McCarthy and Ronan Fitzgerald sat in a private room at the Garrick pub on Chichester Street in Belfast, Northern Ireland. They were waiting for the remaining members of the council of the provision IRA. They had arrived early and were discussing the issues that would be brought up at the meeting.

They were part of the team that had botched the kidnapping attempt on Edward Heath. They wanted to make amends. The city of Belfast allowed them to function easily for it was the home of the movement against London.

Belfast was the capital and the Principal Port of Northern Ireland standing on the banks of the Lagan River and connected through the North Channel to the Irish Sea and to the North Atlantic. It was the second largest city in Ireland. Part of Great Britain in 1800 and in the late 1900's its ship yards were building twenty five percent of British Ships.

Sectarian tensions accompanied the growth of an Irish Catholic population drawn by mill factory employment. There was such a legacy of conflict in the working-class districts of Protestant and Catholic areas that barriers were erected forcing separation. There was uncertainty and anger over Ireland's future in the United Kingdom. From the 1960's when the British army was deployed and the public protests gave way to violence, over 60,000 people were taken from their homes. This was done by the Heath government and their Internment Edict.

This time IRA was successful with their plan. They had abducted Sir Arthur Brooks, one of the most influential persons in the United Kingdom. His ransom would bring 50 million pounds to their depleted coffers. The kidnapping went off just as planned. If Michael Jannsen was there at the time they would have also taken him. There was a security person but he was dealt with easily! Sir Arthur was taken to Belfast quickly and the ransom note went to the States.

When he was taken, they immediately snapped Polaroid photos. The courier took the evening flight to Boston with photos and ransom note, and delivered them the following morning to Michael. In the meantime, Sir Arthur was taken by private plane from London City airport to Belfast. The total operation was seamless, not a glitch anywhere. James Regan and Liam Kelly walked in and had the newspapers under their arms. There wasn't a word in any of the papers. It looked like they didn't contact anyone… or was it just too early.

Conor opened one of the papers.

"I don't think so. I think this Michael Jannsen is a real tough guy. He has a lot of contacts. He is going to try to go about finding Sir Arthur in his own way. This guy looks and feels like trouble. Let's see what happens in the next few hours. It is a little early. Right now, our main task is to leave not a trace of a clue who we are and where Sir Arthur is. We have him here in Belfast and they will have a hard time trying to pinpoint his location; their initial search will be in London's vicinity."

Liam spoke next.

"I want him kept alive and we have nothing if he dies. After we receive the ransom, we will decide his fate. I would like us to get our hands on Mr. Jannsen. That would be a real prize. Now let's talk about the following issues. I want to make sure we follow through on our plans on keepings Sir Arthur well and secure. Let's go over our plan once more."

Ronan added his comments.

"Gentlemen… We want the fifty million pounds. That is the reason for the whole operation. We will not only gain these funds but we will shake the very foundation of Mr. Hearth's administration. We are known rogues to the British, so let us make ourselves unavailable as much as possible until this is over. Now let's talk about the following issues."

Michael was concentrating completely on Sir Arthur.

He had contacted the Mossed and Marcel. Both would meet him in London. He felt like he had to call Edward Heath or possibly fly to London. He knew that to run the operation he had to be there. It could not be done from the states. He assumed that no one knew what happened to Sir Arthur. There were days that he wasn't in the office.

He flew that late afternoon and arrived in London, at 4:30 am. He was in the office by 6:30 am.

Bengy and the London agents of the Mossad were there to meet him at 8:00.

"Gentlemen… I believe the kidnapping is at the hands of the Provisional IRA. If I was a betting man, I would wager they are the culprits. If that is the premise, we have to presume Sir Arthur is somewhere on this island or in Northern Ireland. So, you guys have all sorts of informants and contacts that could lead to his whereabouts. I need you to see what you can do to give us a lead. Let's find this guy."

He called Miss Henley, Sir Arthur's private secretary, and informed her that he was with him and Abe and Sarah Stone. They were on a tour of Stone and Company stores and not to expect Sir Arthur soon.

Bengy picked up the conversation.

"Michael… Have you contacted the British?"

"No, I have not. I plan to speak to Edward Heath, the Prime Minister, in the next hour. Sir Arthur and Heath were not only political allies but also good friends. I will advise you of what we decide. My initial feelings are not to make it public, but to use the powers we have to see if we can find where he is. Marcel Axcel of Axcel industries will be here shortly. We all know who he is and he has had many dealings with the IRA. He could be a real force in finding Sir Arthur."

As Michael finished his thoughts Marcel arrived. Michael explained the situation.

"I am going to let you guys put your heads together. I need to speak and meet with the Prime Minister.

He was able to reach the Prime Minister.

"Mr. Heath, thank you for taking the call. I am in London and I need to speak to you on the subject of the utmost urgency. I don't want to have a phone conversation; is it possible for us to meet as soon as possible?"

"I will make the time. Please come now."

In the Prime Minister's office, Michael explained the situation and told what steps he had taken.

"Mr. Jannsen, I am in full agreement keeping it away from the public. I will assign three people immediately from MI5 to give you all the information we have on this group."

MI5 is the secret service arm that handles threats internally and in Northern Ireland.

"You will have a group of elite army personnel at your disposal if necessary. All our assets are available to bring Sir Arthur home."

"I would like the people to work out of our Fantastique office along with my assets. The melding of their information with the Mossad and Axcel international should make this work."

"Whatever you need. If Scotland yard is necessary, we will bring them into the equation. Please keep me posted on any news."

Michael returned to the Fantastique office and walked into the meeting with Bengy and Marcel. They both had met when they worked out the arms deal. They had some sort of an outline on the black board and explained what they had come up with.

Michael interrupted them.

"Before we go any further, we are going to be joined by three gentlemen from MI5 who should have a significant amount of knowledge about the IRA."

They proceeded to fill Michael in, Bengy seemed to take the lead.

"Presuming we have made the right assumptions that it was the Provisional IRA, this is our game plan.

1 In order for you to receive the letter and photos someone flew from London or Dublin to Boston. We need to check the passenger lists and find that person.

2 We believe Sir Arthur is more than likely in Northern Ireland, specifically Belfast. It would be easier to hide there than in other parts of the U.K.

3 We think he was taken by boat or private plane. We are checking all flights from Heathrow and London City Airports.

4 Marcel has contacts with the Provisional IRA. He has sold weapons to them and will have his people see what they can find.

5 The Mossad have contacts with organizations that share ideology, data, and information that could generate some clues.

6 We want you to check out the staff at Fantastique and see if there are any possible connections with the kidnappings. I believe MI5 can also help you now that they are on board.

7 The information from MI5 can be critical; we will update you as soon as they are part of the discussion.

8 We want you to leave this work to us. We are the pros, so let us do our job."

"Bengy, I am not going away. I am here until Sir Arthur is back sitting at his desk, so let's just get on with it!"

"I thought you would say that."

Michael was worried. Sir Arthur was on certain medications that kept him functioning. He was afraid he could die in their captivity without them.

MI5 arrived with marching orders directly from the Prime Minister. They were given all the information they had acquired on the kidnapping; they in turn gave Bengy and the group their ideas.

"We believe you are on the right track. It is very unlikely that Sir Arthur is in London or on this island. Like you, we believe he is in Northern Ireland. We have already heard rumblings there were plans to bring the Heath government to its knees by some political incident. We have been on alert ever since our informants brought this information to our attention. We will start checking all the flights and possible suspects who would carry the message to the States. We should have a good idea by morning what are some of pieces to this puzzle."

Michael started to check out if there was an in-house connection with his kidnapping.

"Miss Henley, as I said, Sir Arthur is going to be working with me and Mr. and Mrs. Stone in Boston. He will be viewing our major stores on the eastern seaboard. He will not be heard from for a few days."

"I understand. Do you want me to hold his mail. I will list everyone who calls."

"Please handle it as you outlined. I will be spending considerable time here. We need to set up an office next to Sir Arthur's for myself. I believe he started that process.

"Yes, Mr. Jannsen, in fact it's ready now. He rearranged one of the conference rooms."

"I would like to speak to these three people in administration this afternoon."

The interviews were brief. What Michael wanted to see was if anyone was extremely nervous or lied about the last time they had contact with Sir Arthur. One person could be suspect but it was more a shot in the dark. He kept the option open. All the points that Bengy listed were now in play.

The full forces of MI5 were searching the airlines to find the courier. The employee records on all flights from London and Dublin and Belfast from all airports in the U.K. were now being searched. They also reached all their sources of information in the IRA for clues. Marcel Axcel started contacting all his customers. The Mossad used their informants in other revolutionary organizations that had an association with the IRA.

Michael called home.

"My love, how are you doing? The time is growing short and I am not there."

"Michael, do not worry. I am fine. Your family is around me constantly. I am in the best of hands. We all know how urgent this is. We pray every day for his safe return. Take care."

He spoke to Abe and Sarah and filled them in on how they were proceeding. Michael warned Abe that if anyone calls looking for Arthur, he is out viewing the Stone and Co. stores with our real estate people. "Call me if that happens."

CHAPTER
SEVENTEEN

THE WORDS OF Aaron and Joshua were now becoming fact. The news traveled around the world in headlines and news reports. The Yom Kippur war, also known as the Ramadan war, started on October 6th, 1973, between Israel and the Arab coalition led by Egypt and Syria. The war was taking place in the Sinai Peninsula and the Golan Heights, both of which had been annexed by Israel since 1967. The war began when the Arab coalition jointly launched a surprise attack on the Jewish holiday Yom Kippur, which also occurred during the 10th day of the Islamic holy month of Ramadan. Following the outbreak of hostilities, both the United States and the Soviet Union were deeply involved.

Michael followed the news reading every bulletin when he could but his mind was on Sir Arthur Brooks. He was concerned about Aaron and Joshua and how they might be involved in the war. He knew they were also reservists and each led a tank battalion.

Conar McCarthy helped write the details for the 50-million-pound ransom. The instructions were sent to Boston and the Fantastique offices; both arrived by courier. Along with the instructions for payment was an additional note.

"We realize that Sir Arthur has medical issues and have acquired the necessary medications to maintain his health and keep him stabilized. We are only interested in receiving payment as outlined. We have no intention of harming him if our terms are met."

Michael gave the information to the group. He read the new ransom note a number of times and had an idea.

"If they are actually giving Sir Arthur his medication, they have to be acquiring it through a pharmacy, doctor, or clinic. Is it possible to track down where the prescribed medication was ordered in Belfast?

"Can you check all the sources for the medication; it is our only real lead."

MI5 would have the man power to canvas the city. The search was started. At the same time Marcel's contacts had some possible information that verified that Sir Arthur was in Belfast. The IRA was negotiating with the gun merchants to purchase a number of weapons to upgrade their arsenal. It was a purchase that was beyond their usual budget. The negotiators were from Belfast and wanted better weaponry. The Mossad was also in action. They believed Sir Arthur was in Belfast through their informants in their networks.

The instructions were definitely written by a financial person. They were complex. The 50 million pounds would be sent to a number of accounts around the world. They needed to be sent at a certain time and in a certain sequence, Sir Arthur would not be released until they received confirmation that all the transactions went through. Michael was given 10 days to complete the transactions. There were to be no deviations on additional time limits. Any attempt to rescue him would lead to his death.

The instructions were handwritten which was strange. They were printed by more than one person in totally different styles from line to line. The letter was sent to the MI5 laboratory to be analyzed for possible clues. The paper was examined to see where it was purchased to no avail. The courier service was not through normal channels and could not be traced.

Michael given a map of Belfast and with MI5 divided the city into areas they felt would be havens for the Provisional IRA. Michael reviewed the locations and believed these were the areas they should concentrate on. He had MI5 search Sir

Arthur's home and obtained the drugs he was taking. The prescription needed a doctor's authorization. They could now start the search.

In the meantime, the IRA was readying their plans. The Garrick Pub seemed to be a secure place to meet. The pub had a few private rooms for functions. There was a more secure one off of a small office used by the owner Patrick Garrick, who was a third-generation owner. Pat was a member of the IRA and although he was not part of the council, he was an active member. James Regan was the key person in developing the overall plan. He was part of the financial world and outlined how the payments would be made and where the funds would be distributed around the world.

Michael was working from his new office. He had calls coming through for Sir Arthur which were given to him if they were personal. There were many calls of congratulations, some of which he took. He had an open line at all times if the kidnappers wanted to reach him.

Aaron and Joshua were on the line.

"Michael, we are up to our ears with this war; otherwise, we would be there. How is Doria?"

"I realize the situation and appreciate you sending Bengy and the London agents. She is fine and waiting. I will keep you posted."

"We both need a bit of luck."

Michael was starting to receive the war communiqués that Bengy had set up. He read them carefully and was torn that he was not able to contribute. The news was not good.

Golda Meir's decision was not to initiate a war by a pre-emptive strike. Israel needed America's assistance soon and it was imperative that Israel would not be blamed for starting a war. The warnings by the U.S. were very clear. Kissinger and Nixon constantly warned Meir that she must not be responsible for initiating a Middle East war. Israel was dependent on the U.S. Military resupply and sensitive to anything that might endanger that relationship. Kissinger urged the Soviets to use their influence to prevent war. He contacted Egypt with Israel's message of non-preemption and sent messages to other Arab governments to enlist their help. The U.S. was adamant-in demanding that Israel not be the aggressor or the resupplies would stop.

The reports were coming on a regular basis.

The Egyptians had prepared for an assault across the Suez Canal and deployed five divisions totaling 100,000 soldiers, 1,350 tanks, and 2,000 guns and heavy mortars for the onslaught. Facing them were 450 soldiers of the Jerusalem Brigade, spread out in 16 forts along the length of the canal. There were 290 Israeli tanks in all of Sinai, divided into three armored brigades, only one of which was deployed near the canal when hostilities commenced.

Egyptian attack

Anticipating a swift Israeli armored counterattack by three armored divisions, the Egyptians had armed their assault force with large numbers of portable anti-tank weapons, rocket-propelled grenades, and the less numerous but more advanced Sagger guided missiles, which proved devastating to the first Israeli armored counterattacks.

The Sagger missile is an anti-tank missile developed by the Soviet Union. The missile can be fired from portable launchers, vehicles, and helicopters; it has a range of 600 to 900 yards. It has more than reasonable efficiency.

The Egyptians had built separate ramps at the crossing points, reaching as high as21 meters (69 ft) to counter the Israeli sand wall, providing covering fire for the assaulting infantry and to counter the first Israeli armored counterattacks.

The Egyptian Army put great effort into finding a quick and effective way of breaching the Israeli defenses The Israelis had built large 18 meters (59 foot) high sand walls with a 60-degree slope and reinforced with concrete at the water line. Egyptian engineers initially experimented with explosive charges and bulldozers to clear the obstacles, before a junior officer proposed using high pressure water cannons. The water cannons effectively breached the sand walls using water from the canal.

On 6 October, Operation Badr began with a large airstrike. More than 200 Egyptian aircraft conducted simultaneous strikes against three airbases.

Success of the first strike negated the need for a second planned strike. In one notable engagement during this period, a pair of Israeli F-4E Phantoms challenged 28 Egyptian MIGs over Sharm el-Sheikh and within half an hour, shot down seven or eight MIGs with no losses. One of the Egyptian pilots killed was Captain Atef Sadat, President Sadat's half-brother.

Under cover of the initial artillery barrage, the Egyptian assault force of 32,000 infantry began crossing the canal in twelve waves at five separate crossing areas, in what became known as The Crossing. The Egyptians prevented Israeli forces from reinforcing the Bar Lev Line and proceeded to attack the Israeli fortifications. Meanwhile, engineers crossed over to breach the sand wall. The Israeli Air Force conducted air operations to try to prevent the bridges from being erected, but took losses from Egyptian SAM batteries. The air attacks were ineffective overall, as the sectional design of the bridges enabled quick repairs when hit.

There were a whole series of intelligence reports on the Syrian attack in the Golan Heights. Michael quickly glanced at them and realized how serious the situation was in the north. However, he had to concentrate on Arthur at this time.

CHAPTER

EIGHTEEN

THE IRA WAS well prepared for Sir Arthur's arrival. The location they chose was off the Falls Road. It is the main road through West Belfast. The name has been synonymous for many years with the Catholic community in the city. The flat they chose was a short stretch from the city center. They purposely picked it for it was in the heart of the business and retail districts. There was constant traffic and pedestrians; they felt the location would be a great cover for those searching for them. Sir Arthur was taken from home, given a sedative, and driven to a London city Airport. There were two IRA persons in the apartment at all times. They knew Sir Arthur could not and would not attempt an escape. They were there to move him if the need arose.

When he awoke, he asked about Johnson his driver. The answer was not forthcoming. Sir Arthur believed he might have been in on the plot. He always carried a small vial with the necessary medications for a day or two. The kidnappers hired a private plane; the owner was a supporter of the IRA and did not ask any questions. The manifest on his flight information read, "machine parts to Belfast". If he was questioned, it would be very difficult to track for his flight manifests were somehow lost. When they took away Sir Arthur's possessions, they found the medication and asked him to identify the pills. Most of the pills were generic, all except one prescription. Since his diagnosis, most of the medications he took were curtailed. Only one they felt was worth taking. He was not hurt in the abduction and tried to figure out where he was. It didn't take long to hear the unique sound of Northern Ireland.

MI5 had divided Belfast in four zones and sent their teams in to scour the areas for clues. At the same time Michael was hoping one of the groups working to find Sir Arthur would come up with a breakthrough of some kind. They put together a list of the pharmacies that sold this medication in the last few days. It was much longer than they expected. There were 18 pharmacies that sold this drug. It was a start and their only real lead. The group had all the locations on the blackboard and tried to see if there was any way to eliminate some.

Marcel was having a side conversation with Michael.

"Have you any thoughts how they knew of Sir Arthur's schedule or his personal movements?"

"I had a conversation with some of the staff that had worked with Sir Arthur on administrative projects. They all seemed to be above suspicion. The only person who had an intimate knowledge of his movements was his private secretary. She was not a recent employee and had the position for five years replacing his long-time assistant who retired."

"I believe MI5 should check her out if they have not already done so."

MI5 had not finalized their investigation of Miss Henley but had significant information. She was raised in Northern Ireland and has been working in the U.K. here in London for at least 12 years. She was divorced with no children and came to Fantastique with excellent recommendations. Her ex-husband lives in Belfast and as far as they knew was not a member of the IRA. They were continuing to check on his affiliations and movements.

Marcel continued the conversation.

"If you don't object, some of my people could have a private conversation with her. She might have some additional thoughts on the kidnapping; they have a very nice way to make people cooperate."

Michael gave him one of his looks,

"Before we resort to that method let's find out some additional information. I would like to know her financial situation… her latest bank records. Let's call MI5 and they can get us that information within the hour."

Accessing her bank records showed a recent deposit of five hundred pounds. Her monthly salary was significant but not in that category.

Michael discussed the situation with MI5 on how they should proceed. He had some minor dealings with her in all his visits to Fantastique; she would be his personal secretary if he wished. They decided that it might be better if Michael sat down with her and questioned her.

He spoke to her in his new office.

"Miss Henley, you realize something is not right. Sir Arthur is not in the office and can't be reached. What I am about to tell you is strictly confidential and must be treated in that manner."

"There are very few people that know of Sir Arthur's schedule both business wise and personal. We have gone through the list and your name and position stands out as the person who had the most information on his movements and the last to see him in the office.

Do you know where he is?"

She was sobbing.

"I don't know Mr. Jannsen. I gave Mr. Simpson Sir Arthur's personal number and some information for his interview with him and the story he was writing.

"He gave me 150 pounds for giving him the story of the everyday workings of Sir Arthur. I deposited the su with my paycheck of 350 pounds. He was going to write the story from a private secretary's view. He interviewed me for over a half hour about how and when we worked. He gave me his card and asked me to call, if I thought of any other facts that would help the article; he even took a photo of myself for the article. I would never do anything to hurt Sir Arthur."

"Can you give us a description of this person and all that you know?"

She gave them all the facts and MI5 brought her to their offices to see if she could identify possible suspects.

CHAPTER

NINETEEN

THE COMMUNIQUÉS TO Michael were starting to mount.

Battle of the Sinai

On 14 October, the Battle of the Sinai took place. In preparation for the attack, Egypt set down 100 commandos near the Lateral Road to disrupt the Israeli rear. An Israeli reconnaissance unit quickly subdued them, killing 60 and taking numerous prisoners.

The Egyptian Air Force was tasked with their defense against Israeli aerial attacks. Armored and mechanized units initiated the attack on 14 October with artillery support. They were up against 700–750 Israeli tanks.

In the event, the Egyptian armored thrust suffered heavy losses. Egyptian casualties exceeded 1,000. Israel suffered significant losses: 50 tanks and 350 casualties.

Israeli intelligence had also detected signs that the Egyptians were gearing up for a major armored thrust as early as 12 October.

On 16 October, General Sharon dispatched a Brigade to attack the Chinese farm. It was just east of the Suez Canal near an Egyptian agricultural research station. The area was known to the Israeli military as the Chinese farm, a misnomer resulting from the station's use of Japanese-made equipment with Japanese writing on the machinery mistaken by Israeli for Chinese characters. Israeli forces attacked entrenched Egyptian positions overlooking the roads to the Canal. After three days of bitter and close-quarters fighting, the Israelis succeeded in dislodging the numerically superior Egyptian forces.

Israeli breakthrough and crossing of the Suez Canal

At this point, General Sharon advocated an immediate crossing of the Suez Canal. A reconnaissance force had detected a gap between the Egyptian Second and Third Armies in this sector. The gap had been spotted by an American SR-71 spy plane.

On the night of 15 October, 750 paratroopers crossed the canal in rubber dinghies. They were soon joined by tanks, ferried on motorized rafts, and additional infantry. The force encountered no resistance.

On 15 October, Israeli tanks and APCs (Armored Personnel Carriers) crossed the canal and penetrated 12 kilometers (7.5 mi) into Egypt, taking the Egyptians by surprise. By this time, the Syrians no longer posed a threat and the Israelis were able to shift their air power to the south in support of the offensive combination of a weakened Egyptian SAM umbrella.

Israeli jets began attacking Egyptian SAM sites and radar installation, prompting them to withdraw much of the air defense equipment. This in turn gave the IAF still greater freedom to operate in Egyptian airspace. Israeli jets also attacked and destroyed underground communication cables, forcing the Egyptians to transmit selective messages by radio The attack was performed by jets Michael had acquired for Israel.

The Egyptian Air Force attempted to stop IAF sorties and attack Israeli ground forces, but suffered heavy losses in dogfights and from Israeli air defenses, while inflicting light aircraft losses.

The Egyptians' response to the Israeli crossing

The Egyptians, meanwhile, failed to grasp the extent and magnitude of the Israeli crossing. This was partly due to attempts by Egyptian field commanders to withhold reports concerning the Israeli crossing and partly due to a false assumption that the canal crossing was merely a diversion for a major IDF offensive.

After the failure of their counterattacks, the Egyptian General Staff slowly began to realize the magnitude of the Israeli offensive. Early on 18 October, the Soviets showed Sadat satellite imagery of Israeli forces operating on the West Bank of the Canal. Alarmed, Sadat dispatched his Generals to the front to assess the situation first-hand. The High Command recommended that Sadat push forward exploiting their successes.

Israeli forces across the Suez

Israeli forces were by now pouring across the Canal on two bridges, including one of Israeli design, and motorized rafts. Israeli engineers had worked under heavy Egyptian fire to set up the bridges. The crossing was difficult because of Egyptian artillery fire. Sharon's forces on the West Bank launched an offensive. The Israeli forces pushed west toward Cairo.

As the Israelis pushed forward, the Egyptians fought a delaying battle, retreating into defensive positions further north as they came under increasing pressure from the Israeli ground offensive, coupled with airstrikes.

On 22 October, Egyptian defenders were occupying their last line of defense. At around 10:00 am, the Israelis renewed the attack, moving toward the paratroopers who became engaged in intense fighting with their advantageous position. They were able to repel the attack by late afternoon. Meanwhile, the Israelis concentrated artillery and mortar fire against the Egyptian positions.

The Israelis slowly advanced, bypassing Egyptian positions whenever possible. After being denied air support due to the presence of SAM batteries. They also captured Fayid Airport, which was prepared by Israeli crews to serve as a supply base and to fly out wounded soldiers.

CHAPTER

TWENTY

MARCEL HAD DONE all that was asked of him. The Mirages and spare parts had been shipped as planned. The arrangements to move them without being in the public's eye, was essential. The first deliveries of twenty Mirages made a significant difference in the air war especially over Syria. The additional weaponry was essential in the Syrian ground campaigns. The balance of the "shopping list" was being channeled into the war as it arrived. The IAF (Israeli Air Force) had done an incredible job getting the aircraft ready for service. They had arranged for their technicians to accompany the planes on their journey to Israel and performed the necessary services for combat readiness. It saved weeks and was the major difference in the Golan campaign.

Greta was spelling Michael in the product area. Her retail and merchandising filled the gap. With some guidance from Abe and Sarah, she was able to be the decision maker in the line development. She was still nervous over the threats on her life and carried a gun wherever she went. She slept with it under her pillow. She had nightmares of Heinz, her ex-boss's son, attacking her with a knife. The work was her salvation.

Abe and Sarah had their hands full. They were still key executives in Stone and Co. Their experience level acted as the temporary leadership until Michael returned. They all knew what was at stake.

They had made some headway and eliminated many of the possibilities on the black board.

Michael was trying to think as the kidnappers. If I wanted to hide, I would pick the location with the most traffic pedestrians and shopping areas. He did the same in Egypt when we hiding from Nasser. It gave then a natural cover in the midst of everyone.

"Gentlemen, what area in Belfast fits that description. is there a chance that my reasoning is correct?"

He hesitated a moment.

"On the list of pharmacies which sold the mediations are any in the vicinity of the area I am describing?

If so we should be centering our search there."

They immediately went to the board to see if there was a synergy between the two. They found three to four in that vicinity and focused the search in those areas.

Michael phoned Edward Heath,

"Sir, we have some leads and possibilities. We are grateful to you for all your help with MI5 at our disposal.

"Your decision to keep this out of the press has been more than I could've asked for."

"Michael, it serves both our purposes."

Michael had a lengthy conversation with Greta and Abe over a number of issues, it was difficult trying to keep his mind on the business and Sir Arthur.

The council had given Michael ten days to secure and send the funds to the designated entities around the world. They had a meeting on how they would use the funds. They had spoken to a number of gun merchants and were ready to make a sizeable commitment when the money was available. The inquires also included Axcel industries. Marcel's company was asked to price out an extensive package of weapons. Marcel told his lieutenants that he personally wanted to negotiate this transaction. He wanted all the information on the parties involved.

The list of pharmacies was shortening, they had eliminated two of the four and were concentrating on the rest.

Michael had not had an in-depth conversation with Bengy.

"Do you think we are on the right track?"

"I believe we are. All the factors we know point to this location. I believe if we reach the person who picked up the prescription, we will be close to finding Sir Arthur."

"What if we can't find him or her?"

"We will have zeroed in on the area. We will then go house to house and find him."

"This bunch is pretty sophisticated how they snatched him and contacted me. We are dealing with some very clever people. I want you and I to be there when we know where he is."

Bengy raised his voice.

"Michael, I want you to think about letting the pros do their job. Your days of fighting every battle, is over."

"They are, except this one!"

The intelligence reports were more than encouraging.

C H A P T E R

TWENTY-ONE

Egypt's trapped Third Army

KISSINGER FOUND OUT about the Third Army's encirclement. He considered that the situation presented the United States with a tremendous opportunity and that Egypt was dependent on the United States to prevent Israel from destroying its trapped army. The position could be parlayed later into allowing the United States to mediate in the dispute and wean Egypt from Soviet influence. As a result, the United States exerted tremendous pressure on the Israelis to refrain from destroying the trapped army, even threatening to support a UN resolution demanding that the Israelis withdraw to their 22 October positions if they did not allow non-military supplies to reach the army. In a phone call with the Israeli Ambassador, Kissinger told him that the destruction of the Egyptian Third Army "is an option that does not exist."

The Israeli government also had its own motivations for not destroying the Third Army. These included the possibility of using the encircled Third Army as a bargaining chip for ending the Egyptian blockade of the Bab-el-Mandel Straits in the Red Sea and negotiating a repatriation of Israeli prisoners-of- war captured by Egypt. The exhausted state of the IDF, the possibility that humiliating Egypt by destroying the Third Army would make Sadat angrier and unwilling to cease hostilities, and Israel's intense fears that the Soviet Union would militarily intervene were additional reasons for Israel ultimately deciding against destroying it.

Egypt wished to end the war when it realized that the IDF canal crossing offensive could result in a catastrophe The Egyptians' besieged Third Army could not exist without being supplied. The Israeli Army advanced to 100 km (60 miles) from Cairo, which worried Egypt. The Israeli army had open terrain and no opposition to advance further to Cairo. Had they done so, Sadat's rule might have ended.

Michael received the reports on the Syrian front much later and the news was not good. He wished he had been able to replenish the IDF with more anti-tank weapons and tanks to match the bigger and more powerful T-62 which the Russians had provided.

He was hoping that Israeli's ability to outsmart the enemy would win the day.

The Syrians began their attack at 14:00 with an airstrike by about a hundred aircraft and a fifty-minute artillery barrage. The two forward infantry brigades, with tank battalion of each of the three infantry divisions then crossed the cease-fire lines, bypassing United Nations observer posts. They were covered by mobile anti-aircraft batteries, and equipped with bulldozers to fill-in anti-tank ditches, bridge-layer tanks to overcome obstacles and mine-clearance vehicles. These engineering vehicles were priority targets for Israeli tank gunners and took heavy losses, but Syrian infantry at points demolished the tank ditch, allowing their armor to cross.

A Syrian Paratrooper Battalion descended on foot from Mount Hermon and took the Israeli observation base on the southern slope, with its advanced surveillance equipment.

On 9 October, Syrian command committed the Republican Guard Armored Brigade. Fighting in daylight proved to be advantageous to the Syrians: the better armored T-62's were hard to destroy at long range and their high-velocity guns were quite accurate at medium ranges, despite the lack of a rangefinder.

Taking losses and hit by an intense artillery barrage, the Israeli Centurions withdrew from their tank ramps. The situation was restored by an ad hoc force of thirteen tanks from repaired vehicles and stray crews. The Syrians abandoned their last breakthrough attempt, having lost since 6 October some 260 tanks.

Israeli strategic response

Around midnight, the Israelis began to understand the magnitude of the Syrian breakthrough. The entire Golan might be lost. Moshe Dayan decided to personally visit the Northern Command headquarters. In the late night, Dayan was informed that an estimated three hundred Syrian tanks had entered the southern Golan. No reserves were available to stop a Syrian incursion into Galilee. Visibly shaken by this news, the Israeli minister of defense ordered the Jordan bridges to be prepared for detonation.

Next, he contacted Benjamin Peled, commander of the Israeli Air Force. He shocked Peled by announcing that the Third Temple was about to fall. The third temple referred to the Golan falling to the Syrians and possibly the Galilee. It would be as terrible as the destruction of the second temple by the ancient Romans. The IDF had just made a successful start with Operation Tagar, a very complex plan to neutralize the Egyptian AA-missile belt. Overruling objections by Peled, Dayan ordered the destruction of the Syrian SAM-belt, to allow the IDF to halt the Syrian advance.

Less pessimistic than Dayan, General Elazar was not ready yet to abandon the Golan Heights. Israeli High Command had a strategic reserve, Elazar had considered sending this division to the collapsing Sinai front in view of the initial defensive success at the Golan. The unexpected crisis led to an about-face. Priority was given to the north because of its proximity to Israeli population centers at Tiberias, Safed, Haifa, and Netanya. Elazar ordered that, after mobilization, they had to re conquer the southern Golan.

Israeli command feared that the Syrians would quickly exploit this situation by advancing into Galilee. Dayan, in the morning of 7 October, called Shalhevet Freier, the director-general of the Israel Atomic Energy Commission, to a meeting with Golda Meir to discuss the possible arming of nuclear weapons. Meir rejected this option. The Syrian mechanized brigades in this area did not continue the offensive but began to entrench themselves in strong defensive positions. They had been forbidden by Al-Assad to approach the River Jordan, for fear of triggering an Israeli nuclear response. Syria hoped to take the Golan within thirty hours. Coordination with Egypt forced a change of plans. Now uncertain of a successful outcome, the Syrians became less committed to the attack.

Israel retakes the southern Golan

The tide in the Golan began to turn as arriving Israeli reserve forces were able to contain the Syrian advance. Beginning on 8 October, the Israelis began pushing the Syrians back towards the pre-war ceasefire lines, inflicting heavy tank losses. The Israelis, who had suffered heavy casualties during the first three days of fighting, also began relying more heavily on artillery to dislodge the Syrians at long-range.

Israeli advance towards Damascus

A decision now had to be made-whether to stop at the post-1967 border or to continue advancing into Syrian territory. The Israeli High Command spent all of 10 October debating well into the night. Some favored disengagement, which would allow soldiers to be redeployed to the Sinai. Others favored continuing the attack into Syria, towards Damascus, which would knock Syria out of the war; it would also restore Israel's image as the supreme military power in the

Middle East and would give Israel a valuable bargaining chip once the war ended.

Others countered that Syria had strong defenses, such as antitank ditches and minefields, and strong fortifications and that it would be better to fight from defensive positions in the Golan Heights (rather than the flat terrain deeper in Syria) in the event of another war with Syria. However, Prime Minister Golda Meir realized the most crucial point of the whole debate:

It would take four days to shift a division to the Sinai. If the war ended during this period, the war would end with a territorial loss for Israel in the Sinai and no gain in the north—an unmitigated defeat. This was a political matter and her decision was to cross the purple line (the gains the Israelis made after the 1967 war). The attack would be launched the next day, Thursday, 11 October.

On 11 October, Israeli forces pushed into Syria and advanced towards Damascus. They conquered 50 square kilometers of territory. From there, they were able to shell the outskirts of Damascus. The Israeli Army advanced to within 30 km of Damascus. The decision was made to go no further.

CHAPTER

TWENTY-TWO

AARON AND JOSHUA'S roles in the conflict were very different from their normal duties. They were not needed in their international intelligence roles and just like every Israeli of age were assigned to a fighting unit of the I.D.F.

They both were highly trained reservists and held ranks of battalion tank commanders.

When the Syrian's struck in the Golan and vastly outnumbered the Israeli forces, both Aaron and Joshua were called into action to lead their units.

Israeli military intelligence estimated that Syria had over 1,200 tanks. The total division moving forward was 10,000 men. This included a Moroccan brigade.

The Israeli's strategy was to prepare for a counter attack in either the north or the south sector of the Golan. General Ben Gal split his forces to support both areas. As part of the game line, he created a third battalion for maneuvering purposes. Aaron and Joshua had their tank brigades in each sector.

The Syrian northern attack could not be contained, and the Israeli high command made the decision to protect the northern sector for it was more strategic than the southern area. Aaron was in the thick of the fighting.

The Syrians kept advancing and were only held back by Israeli mine fields and tank traps. Aaron's battalion did not have adequate optical equipment for night fighting and had to gauge the position of the Syria forces by their noise and artillery flares. Aaron's ingenuity kept the battalion in the fight by changing positions in order to avoid enemy fire. They were fighting a defensive battle against superior odds.

The Syrians made the mistake of moving too quickly to secure a major cross road. They believed by taking this position the Israeli defenses would collapse.

The Syrian T-55 tanks were equipped with a specially designed infra-red night scope. The night sky was brightly moon lit. Aaron's battalion moved up the valley just near the major road that the Syrians wanted to capture. Aaron's battalion remained silent until the Syrians were in range. When the Syrian tanks were within 800 meters, Aaron and his team opened fire inflicting heavy casualties. After a brief battle, the Syrians retreated.

In the south, Joshua's battalion fought against the Republican Guard which were the elite fighting group of the Syrian army. Joshua had command of seven tanks that held their position in a fire fight and destroyed close to thirty tanks. Later that day, Syrian tank battalions and armored infantry attacked and inflicted heavy casualties on the Israeli brigade.

Joshua was involved in a tank duel that came down to who had the last bullet or shell. The Israelis managed to put together a group of ten tanks. Some of them had only two shells per tank. The call from Israeli command was to hold out for ten more minutes "until we can get you help which is on its way."

What transpired was totally unpredictable. The remaining Israeli tanks had destroyed thirty Syrian T-55s but were completely out of ammunition.

Suddenly, the Syrian forces started to withdraw. The Syrian General Staff had decided to retreat. The Syrian forces had lost over 500 tanks and armored personnel carriers. They were fearful of a possible Israeli counterattack by land and air.

There were over 260 tanks lost in the battle that were lying in the valley. The battle was called the Valley of Tears. The Israelis managed to hold their position and the Syrians withdrew, just as the Israeli defenses were almost to a point of collapse.

Joshua was finally able to call Aaron. "You're on the line so I believe you're okay."

"There was a moment there when I thought I wasn't going to see your lousy face."

"I know the feeling."

Aaron said, "What's left of my battalion is being taken off the line. I will be going back to my usual ho hum job. I guess you will too."

"I guess you're right. After what we've seen, we really never had any excitement."

They both laughed.

The experts were presenting different reasons for the Syrian withdrawal. Some argued that the reason the Syrians stopped was the superiority of the IAF. Michael's contribution of acquiring the Mirages could have made the difference. The Israeli Air Force had the ability to destroy the Syrian ground forces as the Syrians did not have adequate air cover.

CHAPTER

TWENTY-THREE

THE SITUATION IN the Golan had Michael very concerned, he finally felt better when the tide turned and the Syrians were pushed back to the pre-war cease fire line. Reading the reports made him realize how close the Israelis were on the brink of a major disaster. The long list of casualties were beyond his imagination. He had not heard from Aaron and Joshua and was worried for their safety. He wondered if the weapons he and Sir Arthur arranged arrived in time to make a difference. He hoped many were delivered as far as he was concerned; it was too close a call. We were not ready and too complacent. He had heard that story from the boys and wondered what could to be done to rectify the close call.

In the meantime, the emphasis was on Sir Arthur. He had gone ahead and arranged to put together the 50 million pounds if all hope was lost. He believed Arthur would be killed whether they paid the ransom or not, but he felt he had to be prepared to pay, hoping beyond hope that he was wrong. They were getting closer; the clock was ticking on everything meaningful in his life. Doria was about to deliver and Arthur deserved to die in his bed not in the hands of terrorists.

MI5 had now narrowed the list down to two possible people who purchased the medication. The group discussed how they should proceed, without warning the kidnappers. Was the person who purchased the medication an active part of the kidnapping scheme? That was the question on the blackboard. MI5 believed the person was both the purchaser and part of the scheme.

Michael was in agreement, he felt they would not trust a person not in the organization and part of the kidnapping to be involved. The decision now was how to proceed. MI5 outlined who these two persons were. They had done their homework and put together profiles of both individuals. They had the information on the blackboard.

"Here is the first one, her name is Mary O'Malley, Catholic. Her political leanings are definitely with the IRA. Some of her relations were killed in the Derry's Bloody Sunday massacre. For those of you unfamiliar with the event it happened in 1972. British troops fired on protestors in Derry in an area called Bogside. The day became known as Bloody Sunday; twenty-seven civil rights marchers were shot and thirteen died. The army reported the protestors were armed; the evidence shows they were not. It led to an increase in violence as people attacked the army and committed revenge killings."

This brought about the British government to take away power from the Northern Ireland government and began to rule the north directly from London. They called it Direct Rule.

"She knows members, she is divorced and has an ex who works on the docks. As far as we know, he is not politically oriented."

"She bought the medication for a neighbor and had the necessary prescription from a doctor. We have checked with the doctor and he did issue a script for the person the prescription was written for. That is what we have."

Michael looked at the board and remarked

"Where does she work? and what is her education?"

"She works as a waitress and has a high school education as you Americans call it."

There wasn't any other question as they laid out the profile of Aldan Murphy. The M15 agent gave the group his resume.

'He's fifty years old, works on the docks. He does not have any real political affiliation that we know of. He is married with two children and has a medical issue that would demand medication of this kind. What we found out when we started the investigation was that the medication prescribed was more commonly written than we thought. He had been taking this script for the past three years.'

"The pharmacist told us he had a prescription for ten refills; he bought the last over two weeks or ten days earlier than usual. When you look at both profiles there are reasons to choose both as the person we are looking for."

Michael studied them carefully and asked the MI5 group of three what they would do next in order to make a decision.

"If we bring them in for questioning, we will have exposed our presence and any element of surprise. They will move Sir Arthur and we will be as you Americans say… screwed! I believe that that neither one knows the location but they certainly know who knows!!"

Michael replied.

"I believe you have round the clock surveillance of the two. Let's give it twelve-fourteen hours and see if there is a slip up. They may meet up with possible candidates who are either involved in the IRA and specifically in the kidnapping. We need a little luck. The prescription that Aidan picked up was either for him or Sir Arthur. If it was for Sir Arthur, he would need to pick up another shortly for he is overdue. This could be our break."

Michael was right, Aidan Murphy picked up an additional prescription; he told the pharmacist that his wife threw out the medication by mistake.

Bengy, Michael, and MI5 decided on how they would proceed. They wanted to have their "talk" without arousing suspicion.

MI5 arranged with the management of the docks to assign Murphy to a job in a secluded section of a freighter that was unloading cargo.

The group met Aidan as he was about to start working,

"We want to have a talk with you about your medication and why you ordered it twice. We seem to think you had other reasons for the double purchase."

Aidan was nervous.

"I don't know what you mean. I gave the pharmacist the reason for the extra purchase."

The MI5 people conducted the interrogation.

"Mr. Murphy, we want to know who you gave the medication to and we want to under the Internment Rules of 1971. We can arrest you and your family and hold them without trial. Do we make our selves clear?"

Aidan was in tears.

"I was forced to get the medication for them. I do not know anymore. You do not disappoint the IRA. I have seen what happens to those who do not cooperate."

"Who did you pass the medication to?"

"I am a dead man if I tell you. They will kill me and hurt my family."

"How did they know about your medication?"

Aidan hesitated and then couldn't stop talking.

"My brother-in law Liam Kelly asked me for the medication about 10 days ago. He mentioned he needed it for a friend who was arriving from Europe. He told me he was a dear friend and to make sure that when I purchased the medication not to tell anyone. He said our friends are counting on me to help and I should not disappoint them.”

“Do you know where Liam Kelly works and spends time?”

“He also works on the docks on a different shift than I do. I believe he’s a regular at the Garrick Pub.”

Michael drew close to him and grabbed him by the shirt collar.

“Aidan, any word of this comes out of your mouth, you and your family will be jailed as outlined by the Internment Act… and we will throw away the key!

“We need you to go about your work and your family as if nothing ever happened. I am not MI5. I will kill you and your family if you say a word.”

They met to consider their next move.

CHAPTER

TWENTY-FOUR

A MOSSAD REPORT with analyses of the war came through.

The attack into Syria, towards Damascus, would knock Syria out of the war; it would also restore Israel's image as the supreme military power in the Middle East and would give Israel a valuable bargaining chip once the war ended.

The Israeli Navy escorted tankers from the Gulf to Eilat throughout the war, and Israeli tankers sailing from Iran were directed to bypass the Red Sea. As a result of these actions and the failure of Egypt's Mediterranean blockade, the transport of oil, grain, and weapons to Israeli ports was made possible throughout nearly the entire war.

Israel responded with a counter-blockade of Egypt in the Gulf of Suez. The Israeli blockade was enforced by naval vessels based at Sharm el-Sheikh and the Sinai coast facing the Gulf of Suez. The Israeli blockade substantially damaged the Egyptian economy. Throughout the war, the Israeli Navy enjoyed complete command of the seas both in the Mediterranean approaches and in the Gulf of Suez.

U.S.-Soviet naval standoff

The war saw the largest naval confrontation between the United States Navy and Soviet Navy of the entire Cold War. As the United States and Soviet Union supported their respective allies, their fleets in the Mediterranean became increasingly hostile toward each other. The Soviet Operational Squadron had 52 ships in the Mediterranean when the war began. Some carried cruise missiles with nuclear warheads.

As the war continued, both sides reinforced their fleets. The Soviet squadron grew to 97 vessels, while the US Sixth Fleet grew to 60 vessels. Both fleets made preparations for war, and US aircraft conducted reconnaissance over the Soviet fleet. The two fleets began to disengage following the ceasefire.

CHAPTER

TWENTY-FIVE

GRETA WAS WORKING 12-hour days. She had taken over many of the projects that Michael was working on. Her experience overseeing the buying staff in Germany was a great help in working with the merchandisers on the season's purchases. She spoke to Michael daily and followed through as he outlined.

She had certain projects that were near completion that demanded Michael's approval. The sketches and prototypes had to be shown to him.

They both decided she should come to London and finalize the programs. She packed for the trip gun included.

MI5 decided the best way to have their talk with Mr. Kelly was not in the shipyards. He had a shift starting at eleven pm till seven am. They would abduct him just before his arrival for work and inform his superiors he was sick. They would have a minimum of eight hours without anyone knowing his where abouts, and the ability to question him.

The window for the recovery of Sir Arthur was dependent on how cooperative he would be. They were ready to put their plan into action.

The IRA council decided to meet that very night at the Garrick. There were three days left on their 10-day limit for payment.

Sir Arthur was secure in a flat close to the Garrick and under constant guard by two people. They felt the operation had gone off quite well.

In fact, they were optimistic because there was not any public knowledge of the kidnapping.

They felt the new owners of Fantastique and the British government wanted to keep the event away from the press. It gave them a false sense of security on the one hand and a feeling the situation was too good to be true.

Conar addressed the group,

"I do not want to congratulate ourselves just yet, but I believe we could be 50 million pounds richer in three days."

"We shall see very soon."

"We haven't heard a word from them."

"Exactly, we gave them a ten-day window to make the payment. They knew that was more than enough time to arrange the transfer of funds to our designated tax havens. I believe they know that we will not give them an extension. I am not hearing anything negative from our American friends who helped us. Jannsen want Sir Arthur back alive and is willing to pay."

There were a number of comments from the council. Everyone was talking at once; Conar quieted them down.

"We do not intend to send them any additional notes nor speak to them. The less contact we have, the better off we are. Conversation would be the formula for being discovered. We have paid the parties involved in transporting him here. They know what would happen if they exposed us. I've made it very clear to them. We have covered our tracks as best we could. Is there other business…"

"Have we had any pricing on the list of weapons we wish to purchase?"

"Axcel Industries has priced out the machine guns and the grenade launchers."

The IRA council seemed pleased with themselves over the course of events. They all started counting the fifty million pounds.

That same evening MI5 along with Michael and Bengy met at the Fantastique office.

"We now know the person connected to the IRA. He could be part of the terrorists or just a delivery boy. MI5 has given us a profile of Liam Kelly. He had definite links to the IRA and possibly in the hierarchy of the organization. Kelly is more than likely the link to where Sir Arthur is located. He is now under surveillance and we do not want to give him any reason to feel he's being watched."

MI5 had additional people watching the Garrick pub. They felt there were others involved.

"We can possibly come to some additional conclusions; Sir Arthur is probably in the vicinity of the pub. As I said to you previously, the best place to hide is in full view. We need to have a heart-to-heart talk with Liam."

"It will be necessary to be prepared to move quickly, once we obtain the information from him."

MI5 gave their comments.

"He cannot be treated as we handled Aiden. We need to arrange a very private meeting."

"He works the late shift on the dock. It shouldn't be difficult to arrange the same type of meeting. We think it would be easier to isolate him for that friendly chat away from the docks."

Bengy added his remarks.

"We need to be well prepared with a strike team ready to go into action as soon as we know the whereabouts of Sir Arthur. In the meantime, MI5 can get us the information on who comes and goes from the Garrick. I would imagine there are people of interest. My impression is that the Garrick is the headquarters for the Sir Arthur operation. MI5 has seen IRA people coming and going."

"It's starting to get late in the game and time is not on our side; lets arrange that talk with Liam tonight."

Michael was focused on the new evidence from MI5 and additional sources they had acquired. The reports from Bengy were mounting. He glanced at them at first and then become interested when he started to read the latest report. It was quite different than the others and took a totally different reporting approach to explain a very complicated course of events.

CHAPTER

TWENTY-SIX

U.S and Soviet involvement

THE 1973 ARAB-ISRAELI War was a watershed for U.S. foreign policy toward the Middle East. It forced the Nixon administration to realize that Arab frustration over Israel's unwillingness to withdraw from the territories it had occupied in 1967 could have major strategic consequences for the United States. The war thus paved the way for Secretary of State Henry Kissinger's "shuttle diplomacy".

President Richard Nixon came into office convinced that the Arab-Israeli standoff over the fate of the occupied territories could damage America's standing in the Arab world and undermine prospects for U.S.-Soviet détente.

This thinking led Nixon to suspend efforts to reach a settlement with the Soviets and lent credence to National Security Advisor Henry Kissinger's argument that the United States should not push Israel for concessions.

Sadat made two more moves to get the Nixon administration to break the Arab-Israeli stalemate. In July 1972, he decided to expel Soviet military advisors from Egypt, and opened a backchannel to Kissinger. Kissinger was informed that Egypt would be willing to sign a separate peace agreement with Israel that could involve demilitarized zones on both sides of the international border and peacekeepers in sensitive locations. However, Egyptian-Israeli normalization would have to wait until Israel withdrew from all the territories it had conquered in 1967. Secretary-General Leonid Brezhnev, Nixon, and Kissinger believed that given the military balance, Egypt and Syria would not attack Israel, a view supported by much of the U.S. intelligence community.

Kissinger, now both Secretary of State and National Security Advisor, believed that Israel would win quickly. He feared that a rout of the Arabs could force the Soviets to intervene, raising their prestige in the Arab world and damaging détente. He proposed that the United States and the Soviet Union call for an end to the fighting and a return to the 1967 ceasefire lines. The Soviets agreed but the Egyptians rejected a ceasefire proposal. Wanting to avoid an Arab defeat, the Soviets then began to resupply Egypt and Syria with weapons. The Israelis requested that America do the same for them.

The fighting turned against the Arabs. On October 16, IDF units crossed the Suez Canal. Sadat began to show interest in a ceasefire, leading Brezhnev to invite Kissinger to Moscow to negotiate an agreement. A U.S.-Soviet proposal for a ceasefire followed by peace talks was adopted by the UN Security Council as resolution 338.

The 1973 war thus ended in an Israeli victory, but at great cost to the United States. Though the war did not scuttle détente, it nevertheless brought the United States closer to a nuclear confrontation with the Soviet Union than at any point since the Cuban missile crisis. The American military airlift to Israel, moreover, had led Arab oil producers to embargo oil shipments to the United States and some Western European countries, causing international economic upheaval. The stage was set for Kissinger to make a major effort at Arab-Israeli peacemaking.

Michael was totally unaware of these events until he read the report.

He received a message from both Aaron and Joshua. As he read their message, he could read between the lines how relieved they were. He would sense how close the Israelis came to a disaster.

CHAPTER

TWENTY-SEVEN

LIAM KELLY TOOK public transportation to the docks. He could not afford an automobile. The bus stopped about one hundred meters from his destination. There weren't many people at that time of the night. Most of those getting off were headed to the docks. Two MI5 agents had been on the bus before Kelly got on. When they all got off and started walking toward their destinations, the two agents started small talk and asked if he wanted a snort of Irish whiskey before starting his shift.

They stopped along the way in a dark corner; the agent took out the bottle. They handed it to him and at the same time gave him a quick karate chop and loaded him into a waiting black sedan.

If anyone was watching, they saw two men hold their drunken buddy into the vehicle

They did not take him to their office; there were too many eyes always on the law, especially British law.

They brought him to what they called a safe house. He was blind folded the moment he was tossed into the sedan. When they arrived at their destination, they placed a hood over his face.

Michael was waiting at the safe house along with Bengy.

He could see that Kelly was already sweating on a cold, damp evening.

They strapped him to a chair and spotlights were focused on him. The glare would not allow him to see his captures.

They removed the hood and the lights immediately blinded him. He was trying to see who was talking to him, it was not possible. He was hysterical and incoherent.

Michael walked over to him and started to speak,

"Mr. Liam Kelly, I want to introduce myself, I am Michael Jannsen. If you had not heard the name, let me tell you that I am your worst nightmare.

"I am the new owner of Fantastique Ltd. The business was sold to me by Sir Arthur Brooks who I consider a friend, mentor, and comrade in many endeavors. He is part of my family and I would do anything in this world to help him in any situation. We know you have certain information that can rectify the personal situation for Sir Arthur. I want you to know that we must have that information and I will go to any means to get it from you. Do you understand?"

Liam gained some composure.

"Mr. Jannsen, I do not know where Sir Arthur is."

"I don't think you heard what I said. Let me put it a different way."

"What do you mean?"

"Liam, I am not with the British. I am here with my people and we have a different set of rules when we want information; British Law is not in our vocabulary."

"I don't know what you're talking about."

"Let me be a little more descriptive, Mr. Kelly. If you are not forthcoming with what we want to know I will start by cutting off your fingers one at a time. If you do not give us the information, I will cut off your balls and let you bleed to death. Do I make myself clear!"

"So… you have 30 seconds to give us the information we request."

Michael turned to Bengy and the others.

"Gentlemen, strap him down with his hands on the table. So, we can start the procedure. I do not want to hear any more of his B.S."

Bengy and the Mossad agents went about tying him down.

Liam became hysterical, screaming and wetting his pants. He was incoherent.

"Please don't hurt me… I'll tell you. I'm a dead man… please."

Bengy took out a knife that looked like a Bowie knife that could cut through almost any object.

Liam was screaming.

"He's at the Garrick Pub!"

"Liam, we know that is not true."

"My associate will start with your fingers on your right hand."

He screamed.

"He is being held on 21 Divis street on the third floor. Please do not kill me."

"We aren't going to kill you now, but if any part of your story is false, you will die slowly. We need lots more information from you. Anytime you tell a lie you will lose fingers. I said more than one, so tell us what you know. All of it. Let's start from the beginning."

"What is your position in the IRA? Just remember any answer we feel is incorrect, you will lose a finger or two. So, let's hear it now."

"I am part of the council and part of the kidnapping."

"I want to know how you got all the information for the kidnapping. How did you get his personal information?"

"One of our members living in London impersonated a magazine reporter to his personal secretary; she was under the impression that he was writing a story on Sir Arthur."

"How did you know about his medication?"

"When we kidnapped him, we gave him a sedative for the trip to Belfast. We went through his pockets and found the pills; there were only enough for day to two days."

"Who was the key person in the kidnapping?"

"It was Conar McCarthy who dreamed it up. We really wanted Heath but that was a fiasco; we didn't plan it correctly."

"What were your plans if there wasn't payment?"

"I don't know, I guess it would be the decision of the council."

"How is Sir Arthur, is he in decent health?"

"He seemed ok when I saw him last."

"When and why were you there?"

"I did a 12-hour guard duty two days ago. There are two of us with him at all times."

"We want the complete layout of the apartment and who will be there tonight and tomorrow."

Kelly gave them all the information; Bengy drew a diagram of the apartment as he spoke.

"Are the guards armed?"

"Yes, they are."

"Are they experienced with weapons?"

"I don't know."

"When are you due for guard duty again?"

"In two days, it depends on some of us switch shifts."

"Does anyone such as your wife know you are involved in the kidnapping?"

"No, she does not."

"What would be the best time to raid the apartment? I needn't remind you if we do not like your answer…"

"I'm not sure, probably when we are eating. That's the best I can do."

"Who delivered the notes to the States with the Polaroid photos?"

"I don't know his name but he works for British Airways."

"Is there anything else we should know? If something goes wrong with rescuing Sir Arthur, we'll cut off your penis and send you to hell. So, tell us everything!"

"We set up sort of a booby trap on the stairwell leading to the third floor. The third stair from the top of the landing will collapse giving us warning. That is everything I know."

He was crying uncontrollably.

"What is going to happen to me?"

"I haven't decided. It all depends on how we find Sir Arthur. You should start praying that we are successful."

Michael thought that was about all the information they could acquire from Mr. Kelly. They took him away to the other room while they discussed what they just heard.

Michael looked at Bengy.

"Well, what do you think. Did we get what we wanted?"

"I believe we did. Were you ready to cut off his fingers."

"Bengy, I'm not certain, but I brought a sharp knife to make it easy."

Michael hesitated and then spoke.

"You remember what I said to Greta when we told her about the Nazis and needed her help.

She said, "What if I had said no to the proposal."

"I said I would kill you… now let's have some coffee. We need to stay awake. The plan must be in place for the morning."

Sir Arthur was adjusting to the situation as best he could. He spent most of the day resting. The window in his room was blackened so it was impossible to see out. He could hear the noises of a city so he presumed he was in Northern Ireland; he assumed it was Belfast. He had been there several times to see the stores. The voices were definitely Irish. They had given him some magazines to read and fed him fairly well. He had plastic eating utensils and they took his shoe laces away.

It seemed his guards had strict orders not to talk to him. He listened to their conversations which centered around sex and the English Premier League football scores. His thoughts were on what they were asking for his return. Did they contact Michael or the authorities? He did not have any idea what was transpiring. Was Michael leading the investigation? Was there a plan in place to rescue him? All these thoughts were on his mind.

He could not sleep more than two to three hours at a time. They had his medication there when he arrived and he wondered how they received the information. They had given him a disposal razor and shaving cream; it was necessary they were there when he chose to shave.

He sort of lost track of the time and the sedative had disoriented him. Sir Arthur assumed this was his seventh day in captivity. He wondered what Michael was planning. Sir Arthur knew Michael would not sit still because of his past. He ventured to think how he would use all the resources at his disposal. There was hope.

Conar was getting nervous and impatient. His original plan was to have zero contact with Jannsen or the authorities. They had their instructions. Communication verbally was not in their game plan. He would give them one more day to start the process. He believed they would do one or two transactions and wait the full ten days. They would then demand proof of life before proceeding with the balance of the payments.

The good news was they decided to keep this private which meant they were planning to pay. He had a few things to say to the group.

"I believe if we do not hear from them through some transfer of funds by tomorrow, we should consider some changes of plan."

"What changes?"

"We should probably reach Mr. Jannsen and give him a warning. First, we should state again there will not be an extension. If the terms are not met, Sir Arthur's life is in jeopardy."

"I believe we are all in agreement, let's make plans to move him to a new location. We've been in one place too long."

"An excellent Idea."

The council was in consensus.

"Let's use the other flat that we considered before we decided on the current location."

CHAPTER

TWENTY-EIGHT

THERE WERE A number of intelligence reports sitting on Michael's desk that would throw light on the scenes behind the scenes.

U.S intelligence failed to predict the Egyptian-Syrian attack on Israel. On October 4th they continued to believe that an outbreak of major Arab-Israel hostilities was unlikely for the immediate future. When the war started on October 6th, 1973 American intelligence expected the tide of the Yom Kippur war to shift in Israel's favor. They predicted the Arab armies to be defeated in three to four days.

There was a debate in the defense department about whether to supply additional arms to Israel. There was opposition to that move. Kissinger said if the U.S. refused aid to Israel, they would have no reason to conform to an American viewpoint in postwar diplomacy.

On 13 and 15 October, Egyptian air defense radar detected an aircraft at an altitude of 82,000 feet and a speed of Mach 3 (2,300 mph), making it impossible to intercept either by fighter or SAM missiles. The aircraft proceeded to cross the whole of the Canal Zone, the naval ports of the Red Sea, flew over the airbases and air defenses in the Nile delta, and finally disappeared from radar screens over the Mediterranean Sea. The speed and altitude were those of the U.S. SR-71 Blackbird. The intelligence provided by these reconnaissance flights helped the Israelis prepare for the Egyptian attacks.

Aid to Egypt and Syria

Starting on 9 October, the Soviet Union began supplying Egypt and Syria by air and by sea. The Soviets airlifted tons of supplies, of which the bulk of the tonnage went to Egypt; the balance went to Syria and some to Iraq.

Soviet intervention threat

The Yom Kippur war was now in the ceasefire stage. Henry Kissinger mediated a series of exchanges with the Egyptians, Israelis, and the Soviets. On 24 October, Sadat publicly appealed for American and Soviet contingents to oversee the ceasefire; it was quickly rejected in a White House statement. Kissinger also met with Soviet Ambassador Dobrynin to discuss convening a peace conference in Geneva. Later, Brezhnev sent Nixon a "very urgent" letter.

In that letter, Brezhnev began by noting that Israel was continuing to violate the ceasefire and it posed a challenge to both the U.S. and USSR. He stressed the need to "implement" the ceasefire resolution and "invited" the U.S. to join the Soviets "to compel observance of the cease-fire without delay." He then threatened "I will say it straight that if you find it impossible to act jointly with us in this matter, we should be faced with the necessity urgently to consider taking appropriate steps unilaterally. We cannot allow that to happen on the part of Israel."

Kissinger immediately passed the message to White House Chief of Staff Alexander Haig, who met with Nixon for 20 minutes around 10:30 pm, and reportedly empowered Kissinger to take any necessary action. Kissinger immediately called a meeting of senior officials, including Haig, Defense Secretary James Schlesinger, and CIA Director William Colby. The Watergate scandal had reached its apex, and Nixon was so agitated and decomposed that they decided to handle the matter without him.

When Kissinger asked Haig whether [Nixon] should be wakened, the White House chief of staff replied firmly "No." Haig clearly shared Kissinger's feelings that Nixon was in no shape to make major decisions.

The meeting produced a conciliatory response, which was sent in Nixon's name. At the same time, it was decided to increase the DEFCON from four to three. Lastly, they approved a message to Sadat (again, in Nixon's name) asking him to drop his request for Soviet assistance, and threatening that if the Soviets were to intervene, so would the United States.

DEFCON defense readiness condition is an alert state used by the U.S. Army ranging from DEFCON4 to DEFCON1. It indicates how severe the situation could be. DEFCON3 is a state of heightened rapidness. It meant the air force would be prepared to fly in fifteen minutes.

We have only reached DEFCON2 during the Cuban missile crisis.

The Soviets placed seven airborne divisions on alert and airlift was marshaled to transport them to the Middle East.

The Soviets quickly detected the increased American defense condition, and were astonished and bewildered at the response. "Who could have imagined the Americans would be so easily frightened," said Nikolai Podgorny. "It is not reasonable to become engaged in a war with the United States because of Egypt and Syria," said Premier Alexei Kosygin, while KGB chief Yuri Andropov added that "We shall not unleash the Third World War." The letter from the U.S. cabinet arrived during the meeting. Brezhnev decided that the Americans were too nervous, and that the best course of action would be to wait to reply. The next morning, the Egyptians agreed to the American suggestion, and dropped their request for assistance from the Soviets, bringing the crisis to an end.

Michae actually went over sections of the report again. He was astonished by the content and in somewhat disbelief of the results. It was a world he wanted no part in.

CHAPTER

TWENTY-NINE

IT WAS ONE o'clock in the morning when they had finished with Liam. Michael, Bengy, and MI5 kicked around how they should proceed.

Michael brought the meeting in order.

"Liam's shift is to 7:00 am this morning and we can assume we have at least to 10:00 am to consider that anyone would consider him is missing."

"Is there any way to extend that period till 1:00 pm?"

MI5 continued the conversation

"It may not be a problem. His wife works and the children are in school. He generally goes home to sleep. I believe we can safely say he will not be missed until later in the day. Our shadowing him for the past days bears that out."

"If that is the case we should make our plans accordingly."

"How many men do we need for the operation?"

"I believe five seasoned men should be sufficient."

Michael said,

"Does that include myself?"

"No, Sir, it does not include you. I believe you should leave the operation to the professionals."

Michael stood up and walked over to the window.

"I understand your position and concern, but I will be with you, so let's not waste our time discussing it any further."

Bengy got involved.

"I imagine we will keep Mr. Kelly here until the operation is finished! We need the element of complete surprise."

MI5 brought over a detailed map of the area and showed Michael and Bengy exactly where Sir Arthur was being held.

"He's on twenty-one Divis street. It is in the middle of the block. The street has traffic but not continuous. We do not think we should arrive by auto. We would split into two groups entering the street from two different locations. We don't want one of the guards looking out the window and seeing a group of us getting out of cars. We will have cars around the corner at the end of the street. They will appear when we heave Sir Arthur out the front door."

"Should we have anyone posted on the street if by some chance their comrades arrive?"

"We will have two people on the opposite side of the street who will be walking toward the location."

Michael asked,

"What kind of weapons will you use if necessary?"

"All of us will have revolvers; two of us will have machine pistols that have multiple rounds. One of us will have an axe to break down the door. We will announce our presence in that manner if necessary. Generally, it is much simpler to break down the door in these old buildings with your shoulder."

"The operation is based on surprise. The major problem we have is entering the building. There are three floors and Sir Arthur is on the third floor. We presume the main entrance is open."

Michael heard the plan and looked at Bengy.

"What do you think?"

"I don't like it."

"What's wrong with it."

"We need a better approach to the house."

"How would you do it?"

"I would use one of the city's vehicles that service either the electrical or gas repairs. The truck would pull up to the building and two workmen would approach the residence. They would have reason to enter. They would be dressed in work clothes. Their excuse would be an electrical issue or gas leak or just maintenance. They could ring the bell of the first-floor apartment to gain entrance if necessary. The rest of the plan is fine. The other agents would follow as you laid out. Entering would be a lot less noticeable."

They all decided this was a better course of action. MI5 got busy to make the arrangements.

In the same time frame, Greta arrived on British airways and made her way to the hotel. Michael wanted her to stay at the Connaught where he was staying. She had taken a night flight and by the time she went through customs and a taxi from Heathrow to Mayfair it was 9:00 am. She checked into the hotel and called Fantastique looking for Michael. The switch board transferred her to a voice message that Michael had left.

He gave her instructions to meet with the Fantastique design staff and see what they were working on. He would catch up with her later. She should take the day off or shop the city. Greta knew the shopping areas of London extremely well. London was the fashion leader in young and fashion apparel. That was the strength of Kaufhaus where she was the fashion director. She shopped the London boutiques on a regular basis.

She was not tired and spent most of the day shopping Knights Bridge and Kings Row and Harrods's. She knew Michael had shopped Selfridge's. Greta's jetlag was kicking in so she worked her way back to the hotel. As she stopped to look at a window, she was greeted in German. She looked around and two of her buyers from Kaufhaus were there and so happy to see her. She had left her position of creative director almost overnight and never explained anything to her staff. They had suggested coffee and Greta agreed. Greta didn't have to ask any questions. The buyers gave her a full report of what was happening. They both asked her if there were any opening in her new position. Both were looking to leave Kaufhaus.

Greta did not have to ask any questions. She just sat and listened. Heinz Adler didn't come up in the conversation. They parted and she told them where she could be reached in London and the States. Greta had dinner in the dining room in the hotel. She left a message for Michael hoping he would join her.

The group went over all the details and MI5 showed them photos and diagram of the street. Their men would be in position at both ends of the block and converge on the building at the given time. Michael insisted that he be part of the attack force. He was the only one outside of Bengy who knew Sir Arthur.

The weather was cold and damp and fog covered the city. It was almost lunch time and there was a decent amount of traffic. The noises of the city could be heard: Delivery trucks and pedestrian traffic, the normal sounds that were the noise of Divis street. MI5 had coordinated their movements and the operation went into effect as the electric company truck came down the street.

It was slowed down by the traffic and inched forward stopping at number 21 Divis. There was nothing unusual happening. The everyday workings of the city were in play. The workmen got out and went to the back of the truck and took out their kits; they had their handguns under their work jackets and machine pistols in their work boxes.

On the third floor the two guards were getting their lunch in order. Conar kept a flat on the second floor and came upstairs to check everything.

"How have things been going? How is our patient?"

"He seems to be all right. We don't talk to him. Those are your orders."

"We are getting lunch ready. Do you want some stew?"

"No, I will eat later. I'm just concerned about the plan. I've got a bad feeling they are hatching some sort of plan. As I said at the meeting we are going to move tomorrow. I would like to do it today but the new flat won't be ready till then. I just want to go over the plan if anyone tries to rescue him. We know what to do."

"Just to be sure… At the first sign of an attempt I want you to do as we planned. You are to open the door built in to the floor and send him down to my flat once you have the slide in place. Just slide him down. If that is not possible, kill him. I'll check on you later before the next shift comes."

The MI5 men came to the door and didn't need to ring the bell. The front door was ajar and they entered the hallway. There was a woman about to enter her first floor flat.

"You gentlemen, what are you doing here?"

"We need to check the wiring in the building. We will start on the third floor and work our way down. You can expect us later."

Michael and the other MI5 men were on their way to the front door. They started slowly mounting the stairs and left their kits on the landing, the machine pistols in hand.

Sir Arthur heard the conversation and felt the situation was hopeless. He had hoped the last five months of his life would be spent seeing friends and helping Michael. The kidnapping had taken its toll. He did not have the strength to mount any kind of defense. His jailers were nervous. They were going to move him tomorrow and that would mean there was little hope of a rescue. He knew once the ransom was paid, they would kill him. He asked for pencil and paper, so that he could write some of his thoughts to Michael and the world. He had little hope that it would be delivered.

They brought him his Irish stew and said nothing as always. He heard the plan, if there was an attempted rescue. They had built an opening in the floor between the flat and had some sort of a rigged slide set up so they could move him down to the lower level. They must have some warning system in place to give them the time to get this done. He did not know of the rigged third step which would give them warning.

What could he do if there was a rescue attempt. He could push the bed against the door and hold them for taking him for a minute or two. There was a basin in the room for him to wash. He could fill it with hot water and throw it in their faces. That would take time but was possible. There was nothing else in the room that could be used as a defense. All he felt was despair.

While these events were occurring, the intelligence briefings and records were mounting on Michael's desk.

U.N. backed cease fire

On Oct 25th the United Nations Security Council passed resolution 338 in order to bring a cease fire in the Yom Kippur War. There was a four joint proposal by the United States and the Soviet Union. It was passed by the Security Council by fourteen votes to none, with China abstaining.

The resolution stipulated that the ceasefire should take effect within twelve hours of the adopted resolution. It outlined that negotiation process should start between the Arab States and Israel. Fighting continued despite passing resolution 338 and the Security Council.

Resolution 339 was adopted on 23rd of October in order to end the war, where resolution 338, two days before had failed.

The resolution primarily reaffirmed the terms outlined in 338; returning both sides back to when the position came into effect. It also spelled out measures towards the placement of U.N. observers to supervise the ceasefire. Most heavy fighting on the Egyptian front ended shortly after; there were still clashes along the ceasefire lines and some air strikes on the encircled Egyptian third army. Egyptian national security advisor sent Kissinger a stunning message: Egypt was willing to enter into direct talks with Israel, provided that Israel agrees to allow non-military supplies to reach the third army and to complete a ceasefire. Israel had completely encircled the Egyptian third army of 30,000 men and had the power to destroy it.

On 25th of October, Kissinger appeared before the press at the State Department. His remarks spelled out the principles of a new U.S. policy toward the Arab-Israeli conflict. He made the following statement.

"Our position is that… The conditions that produced this war were clearly intolerable to the Arab nations and that in the process of negotiations it will be necessary to make substantial concessions. The problem will be to relate the Arab concern for the sovereignty over the territories to the Israeli concern for secure boundaries. We believe that the process of negotiations between the parties is an essential component of this."

C H A P T E R

THIRTY

THE APARTMENT BUILDING at 21 Divis street had four units per floor; it was the typical structure in this Belfast neighborhood. It needed repair which was visible when one entered the hallway. The plaster and paint were peeling and it needed carpentry work on railings on the stairways. There was a musty odor and the scents from breakfast of the Ulster fry lingered in the hallway. They were accompanied by the aromas of potato and soda bread being made for lunch.

The two MI5 workmen started to climb the stairs to the second floor.

Conar was exiting the third floor and was on his way down to his flat. He sensed something was wrong as he looked down the stair well and saw the two so-called work men machine pistols in hand.

He backed up and started to work his way back to the third floor.

The MI5 Team started converging from both ends of the street

Michael was now at the door way and entered with two additional MI5 operatives.

Conar rushed to the third floor flat and startled the two guards.

He motioned for them to be quiet and quickly told them that he was certain there was a rescue team for Sir Arthur mounting the stairs.

Sir Arthur realized there was something happening for it was too quiet in the flat. He could hear that Conar had returned. Could there be a rescue in process. It was possible. He had to get ready and do his part.

Conar motioned to them to open the floor door and get ready to bring Sir Arthur out so he can slide down to his flat. The plan was when he was in their grasp and ready to slide down, Conar would go first and then receive Sir Arthur.

Before Sir Arthur could do anything, they took him from the room, tied a bandana on his mouth, and cuffed his hands in front of him.

Sir Arthur didn't struggle. He didn't have the strength. Conar slid down to second floor and then motioned the two to put him on the slide and push him down.

Their instructions were to close the opening and place the rug back on the spot and wait for the law to enter. They were to do nothing… say nothing… they knew nothing regarding the kidnapping.

Conar now had Sir Arthur and put him in a closet unable to speak and cuffed.

Conar gave him instructions.

"Sir Arthur, if you make any noise, I will not hesitate to fire into the closet."

MI5 worked their way up the stairs and avoided the third stair from the landing as they learned from Liam Kelly.

Conar took the slide down and placed it in the other room, he sat there waiting for the rescuers to search the flats. He was counting on them to search his place and not open every dresser drawer or closet.

He thought they must have gotten their information from one or two sources, either Liam Kelly or Sean Driscoll. Those were the only two that could have given them the precise location. If his luck held, they would abandon the search and believe he had been moved. He was thinking ahead of when and how he should move Sir Arthur. This neighborhood would be inundated with Brits from every agency.

It would not be easy to move him to the next location. He did not want to kill him for the 50 million pounds would give them all the funds they need to fund a revolution.

Conar was not going to do anything rash unless he absolutely had too.

He could hear the MI5 people breaking down the third-floor door. His compatriots were setting at the table eating their Irish stew.

The two MI5 men who had burst into the flat guns drawn were stunned to see the two men sitting at the kitchen table eating. They were followed by Michael, Bengy, and then by the MI5 people. The bedrooms were searched and nothing was found.

Michael entered the flat and surveyed the scene.

Two guards sitting at the table eating their lunch without a care in the world. Something was dramatically wrong.

The first thing in his head was that he could swear Liam Kelly gave them the correct information. What went wrong? He turned to Bengy.

"Well, what do you think happened?"

"Michael, I don't know how they accomplished the escape. I would swear that Kelly gave us the correct information."

"I do too. Did he omit telling us everything or did we screw up?"

"I think it was some of each."

MI5 will search the entire building. I doubt if they find anything.

Michael added,

"I want to be in on the interrogation of these two. They seem to be too confident and at the same time did you notice they were sweating on a cold day."

"You could be right. We need to have another heart-to-heart talk with Kelly."

The MI5 group came back and confirmed that Sir Arthur was not in the building. They had done a routine search of each flat.

Michael asked the MI5 men the following,

"Are their members of the IRA living in the building. Let's check that out. I do not believe we have that information."

Michael continued the conversation with Bengy.

"Some of the answers are here. I am not willing to write this place off the list."

Conor had weathered the storm. The MI5 searched the flat but not thoroughly. He felt a sense of relief for the time being. He took Sir Arthur out from the closet and chained him to the bed in the second bedroom. Sir Arthur was exhausted and bruised from the slide and being tossed around. He had heard people entering the flat but could not make himself heard with the bandana on his mouth. He was totally exhausted and had lost all faith in being rescued. Sir Arthur thought he might be released if the ransom was paid but that was highly unlikely.

Conar had to come up with a new plan on how to move Sir Arthur. He was stuck in the fiat. MI5 had forbidden anyone to enter 21 Divis street that wasn't a resident. He could not leave him alone. He had the phone but was afraid MI5 would tap all the lines. Any conversations had to be normal routine talk. Maybe it was possible to make his comrades understand.

Michael was perplexed with the situation and spoke to MI5.

"I am of the opinion that there are other individuals in the building that have information about Sir Arthur. We should keep a close watch on the residents, and study their actions. I believe you are going to monitor their phone lines?"

"Yes, we are, and check each individual out in regards to political leanings."

"You will keep me posted."

Michael was exhausted and went back to the hotel. It was late and there was a message from Greta. He had forgotten with all that transpired that she had come to London to show him the final sketches and development for the season. There were also messages from Aaron and Joshua that he needed to address. All the balls were in the air and none could be set aside. They were all in play. It was only 6:00 pm in Boston and he called Doria.

"My love, how are you feeling? What did the doctor say? I believe you saw her today."

"I'm right on schedule, everything seems to be working. Please don't worry, I am doing well and we will be okay. The family is here with me and everyone sends their love. How are things progressing? Is there any more word on Sir Arthur?"

"Nothing as of now, my love. It is late here and I am exhausted, I'll talk to you tomorrow."

Michael met with Greta for breakfast and spent an hour or more going over the program. He asked her to go ahead to the office and get started the on the programs. He would join her later. He had her send a telex to Aaron and Joshua that he would speak to them later. He met up with Bengy at MI5 headquarters. He wanted to do the following!

1. Speak to Liam Kelly
2. Go over the information on those residing at 21 Divis street.

Liam Kelly was being held under the Internment Act that Edward Heath had instituted. It allowed him to be held with no explanation or crime.

Michael started the conversation,

"Liam, you're a very fortunate man that you are in the custody of the British."

"Why is that?"

"Because if you were under my jurisdiction, you would be minus a number of fingers or more."

"I gave you everything I knew. They are going to murder me and my family when I am released."

"You didn't tell us everything, otherwise we would have rescued Sir Arthur Brooks. I want to go over your whole story again. Something is not right and you have the answer we are looking for."

"I don't know any more than I told you and I am not about to squeal on any of my brothers in arms."

Michael realized this was a dead end and he needed to look elsewhere.

"Liam, we are not going to let you go. We will give the complete story to the press which should make you very popular with your brothers in arms."

"You are signing my death warrant."

"If you do not want this to happen, you can play ball as we Americans say, and tell us all you know about the organization. The MI5 people are standing by to hear your story. We want names of all your group leaders and those involved in the kidnapping… Now!"

Conar was contemplating how he could possibly get Sir Arthur out of the building. The MI5 and police had roped off the entire area and were conducting their investigations. Sooner or later, they would find out who he was. He felt he had a day or two at the most to make his escape with Sir Arthur. He needed a plan that would bring them both to safety.

MI5 was in the process of reviewing the information on the residents or families at 21 Divis St. Most of the residents were unknown to MI5 and it would take some time to gather information on each subject. There were at least two to four residents in each unit, not counting the children. They had at least twenty-five people to review. Liam Kelly did give them names and MI5 went into action and started to round up the three to four people who were part of the kidnapping. They were not the key participants but those who worked the connection.

Conar came up with a plan. It was rather unique and demanded coordination with a number of sources. If he could line them up, there was a good possibility that both he and Sir Arthur could escape the net around the building. When MI5 questioned him, he told them his wife and mother were shopping and his two children were in school. Actually, they all lived in another section of Belfast. He was worried they would discover the flat. IRA had rented the second floor so they would have an alternate escape route. They would find out soon that he did not live there.

Conar reached a doctor who worked with the IRA.

"Doctor, my mother is not doing well and it is impossible to move her. I believe her condition is serious. Is it possible for you to come over as soon as possible."

"Mr. Conar, I will be there this afternoon. Please do the following until I get there."

The doctor was able to enter the building after he answered questions why he was here. He met with Conar and discussed how they were going to move the "patient" to the hospital. I am currently off duty so it would be unwise to ask my hospital staff for an ambulance. It will need to be done tomorrow. I will return here and find the patient needs immediate medical care at the hospital and order an ambulance; this is the best option.

Conar reluctantly agreed. He wanted to move as quickly as possible. He had no other option.

Michael and Bengy went over all the details again. Michael was looking at some of the information on the tenants. The information revealed there were several people who could have an association with the IRA. They needed to be checked out.

"We should accompany MI5 when they do the interviews and get it done as soon as possible. The longer we wait the trail gets colder."

"I agree. Let's push MI5 to get started today."

They both went back to Divis street. John Singlewood, an MI5 inspector who had come over from London to help with the investigation, was sent personally by Edward Heath. He was in contact with Michael on how the search was going.

"We really need to clear up any questions we have with the residents."

"We all are in agreement. There are three potential persons who could be involved. The first two were relatively easy to eliminate. One was in a wheel chair and the other was 80 years old."

The doctor arrived early and Conar brought him into Sir Arthur's room,

"Conar, in order to move him, we will need to give him a shot. It should keep him asleep for three to five hours depending on his metabolism. Once he is asleep, he will be easy to move with the orderlies in the ambulance. I have scheduled the ambulance for arrival in about one-half hour. What are your plans?"

"We can bring him to a clinic where there are friends of the organization and then you can make other arrangements. I believe this is the best solution."

"Your plan seems to work. I can move him to a secure location from that point. I cannot make further plans until I leave."

"You will ride with the patient which is quite normal."

"We have everything in place."

They had finished interviewing the tenants on the first floor. The others who were in question were on the second floor. Michael noticed the number of the flat. It was exactly under the unit where they were holding Sir Arthur. He mentioned it to Bengy who didn't believe in coincidences.

When they arrived at the door, they knocked and rang the bell. They were about to force entry when the woman in the next flat came out.

"They aren't home. They just took someone to the hospital in an ambulance. I saw them go down the stairs just before you came."

Before she finished her sentence, they were down the stairs and looking for the ambulance.

Singlewood from MI5 had his sedan parked in front of the building and they were immediately moving down the street.

He radioed the agents on the street and received confirmation that the ambulance had turned the corner at the end of the street, moving toward the Falls Road. It was more than likely heading on to the A501 running southwest. They had them in sight. The plan was to follow the ambulance. They did not want to confront the assailants now for fear they would kill Sir Arthur.

Singlewood was on the radio to get all the information he could on the ambulance and Conar. His name was on the rental lease. They continued to follow the ambulance at a sufficient distance.

CHAPTER
THIRTY-ONE

CONOR RODE IN the back of the ambulance with Sir Arthur and the doctor. They were not able to see if anyone was following them. The ambulance's back window was small. The ambulance sped down the A501 and after five miles turned on to a side road which turned out to be an old estate that was converted to a private clinic.

Singlewood received the information on the clinic. The dossier on Conar McCarthy came in; he had a connection to the IRA and at one time was held for interrogation but never jailed. The ambulance pulled up to the entrance, and they transported the patient inside. Michael and Bengy watched Sir Arthur being brought into the clinic. They needed to finalize a plan that would not cause Sir Arthur's death.

Michael gave his opinion.

"I do not think they plan to keep him here. Somehow, I believe this is a temporary stop. This clinic as you explained has a triple A rating and would not willingly harbor this kidnapping. They have gone to great lengths to keep Sir Arthur alive. I believe they are going to try to reach me and push for payment. We don't have a lot of time because of Sir Arthur's condition. We will need to move within the next few hours at the most."

Singlewood had radioed for additional agents. When they arrived, they situated themselves in the bushes around the clinic after discussing the strategy with MI5 and Michael.

Michael was in full agreement.

"If we screw up, he's dead. We are only going to get one chance."

They had a basic layout of the clinic. One of the agents brought it. MI5 presumed that he was being held in some waiting area and not with the patients. They were assuming this was the case. The facility had an area for arriving patients, where they were assigned until they were given an actual room.

Their strategy was based on this assumption and the plan was discussed.

Michael and Bengy were in agreement.

MI5 wanted to move immediately.

Michael spoke up.

"Gentlemen, Sir Arthur is not in serious trouble as of now. He will be if we attack. I would like to wait an hour and see if the IRA makes a move to move him to their safe house. If they do, let's make our move when they make the transfer. We should get out of sight and see if this will happen. If nothing happens soon, then let's put the plan in action."

They all agreed.

When Conar had the patient in place, he immediately called his people to come and pick up the patient and himself.

"How long will it take you to arrange a large car to take us to our new destination?"

"We should be there in a little more than an hour."

Conar started to relax. He felt he had outwitted the Brits. When he had everything in order, he would reach this Jannsen person to seal the payments. He believed they would now pay.

Sir Arthur had awakened from his shot. He felt the bruises of being tossed around, but he was alive. They had moved him but where?

He looked around and thought he was in a hospital; everything was hazy and the room seemed to be moving. He thought why a hospital, was he free? He realized he was still cuffed, where was he? He tried to determine what happened.

Conar and the doctor came into the holding area where he was kept.

Conar was pleased and spoke to the doctor.

"I appreciate all that you have done. I would like you to check him out. I have his medication that he takes on a regular basis. We are going to move him shortly to our safe house."

The doctor checked Sir Arthur's vital signs.

"He is in stable condition for the time being. I would not move him again. His overall condition is not normal."

"We are only going to move him once more. We need him alive because the parties want proof of life. The move takes place within the hour."

Michael and MI5 saw two cars coming up the driveway from their vantage point. His prediction was right. They came to move him. There were two men in each car as they started to pull up to the entrance. MI5 had the agents in the bushes. When they came out of the cars, they were greeted with guns in their faces. The pairs in the second car drew their pistols and a hail of bullets resulted in both men down on the ground.

Michael had hoped this would not be the case. The element of surprise no longer was in play. All IRA members were down, some mortally wounded, one of the MI5 agents was slightly wounded but not life threatening. Conar and the doctor reacted immediately by barricading themselves in the anti-room with Sir Arthur.

"They won't rush us; we have Sir Arthur and they want him alive."

"Conar, said the doctor, "I don't want to be involved; I did my part for the organization. I am not part of the kidnapping. I thought I was moving a patient to a clinic. I want to surrender to the authorities and tell them I was not involved politically."

"You're in it up to your eyeballs. You are not going to get a free pass. So, stop this bull shit and keep quiet while I figure out what we should do."

Michael, Bengy, and the MI5 met to decide their next course of action.

Michael was right to the point.

"We need to move quickly. Sir Arthur needs medical attention.

"He can't continually take what is happening. He was weak to begin this ordeal. There must be other entrances to the clinic. We need to know exactly where he is being held and then move against them."

They found the entrance on the side of the clinic. There was turmoil in the building caused by the gun shots. There weren't that many patients and staff but they were huddled in the dining room not knowing what to do.

The MI5 agents led them out of the building.

Michael and Bengy listened to the plan that Singlewood had devised. His strategy was to fill the area with smoke grenades. He suggested using the bursting variation, the smoke is spread quickly into a cloud. It produces a very dense and an instantaneous cloud of white smoke. It should be very effective. They do not directly emit sparks or a fire hazard.

"I believe this is our way to enter the area where they are holding Sir Arthur."

Michael and Bengy were in agreement,

Sir Arthur heard the shots; there was hope. He tried to move and see what was happening. He was lying on a cot in the corner of the room. There were two men in the room. He was still half awake from the injection. The MI5 had set up a speaker.

"Conar McCarthy, we have captured or killed your IRA associates that came to help you. You have no means of escape. Come out with your associate, hands over your head."

"You MI5 bastards… I will kill Sir Arthur Brooks if you attempt to enter. I want safe passage or he dies. I have a doctor here who is keeping him alive. If you do not arrange a car for us, you know the answer. I will give you one hour."

They did not have a choice. They had to make the rescue attempt now. It was getting dark and Michael had an idea.

"Do you have night vision goggles available? If so, we should shut the power off and use the smoke and the darkness to strike."

Bengy laid out his plan.

"Don't shut the power off but turn it off and on for thirty seconds. Then shut it off. It will create havoc and disorient them. We will then use our night vision goggles and have a distinct advantage. We will need to coordinate the timing."

The room where they held Sir Arthur had one window. The smoke grenades would be launched into the room as planned in conjunction with the lights blinking. Everyone was in position. They had set their watches to coordinate the smoke grenades, the lights, and the actual assault.

Michael and Bengy insisted they be part of the rescue team. They were to be four in total entering. They had a battering ram. The key was to have all the elements of the siege to go off in the right sequence.

Michael and Bengy positioned themselves on the side of the MI5 agent who would batter down the door.

They had a drawing of the room where they thought Sir Arthur was held. The clinic supervisor had given them the information and identified the area in the room where he would possibly be on a bed or chair.

They were to start the assault as soon as the smoke grenades went into action, which was almost instantaneously. They heard the glass breaking and the door gave way quite easily. The smoke grenades were working. They had their night goggles on and the blinking lights strategy was creating issues in every way. Conar had his pistol out and shot widely at what he thought were figures in sight.

Michael headed for the corner of the room where they thought Sir Arthur would be. The doctor was blocking him and at the same time trying to avoid the dense smoke. Michael with gun drawn didn't shoot but used the butt handle to smash him across the face. He immediately fell to the floor.

The smoke was extremely dense and it was easy to lose one's perspective. He thought he could see a metal headboard and was hoping it was where Sir Arthur was bedded. At that instance, a bullet lodged in the wall beside him. He turned to see Conar McCarthy preparing to fire again. The smoke must have disoriented him for his next shot was not in his vicinity. In the next instance he saw Conar go down and agent Singlewood stepped out of the smoke.

"I really didn't have a choice. He would have killed you."

Sir Arthur was in the bed at the corner of the room as they had thought. He had closed his eyes when the smoke was upon him. He lay there thinking there was a glimmer of hope that he would live through this day. He was aching from all the movement he had to endure, and was still somewhat in a fog. Reality was somewhere out there in the smoke. His mind was wandering through the years; it seemed as if he was living in a dream. Was this the way he would die in a room filled with smoke and the sound of gun fire? Or was he going to be rescued from this inferno. Out of the mist came a figure who looked like someone from another planet. Was he hallucinating?

The tall dark men took off his mask and embraced him.

"Oh, my God, it's you. Michael, where and how did you find me?"

"Never mind the questions. We need to get you to the hospital and check you out. We have an ambulance on its way. I will ride with you. Bengy and I have been looking for you for quite some time. We are not going to let you out of our sight.

"We were all concerned about you. I told Doria she couldn't have our baby until you were there for the Bris (a circumcision)."

Sir Arthur started to cry.

"Michael, what would I do without you."

"I think you have done fairly well for 68 years... and counting."

The ambulance came and they brought him to the hospital.

"What happened to the persons who had me captive?"

"Most of them have been dealt with one way or another."

"How is the war going?"

"I don't have all the information. I have been busy with you. It seems we dodged a bullet. We survived but not unscarred.

"We need to get you well, so I can ask you a million questions about Fantastique. That's the reason I went looking for you."

"I assumed the same."

They both laughed,

"What about our project with Marcel. Did it come to fruition?"

"Yes, it was successful, enough for today. We will talk later. Try to rest."

Michael got to a phone and called Doria. It was just about dinner time in the States.

"My love, I have great news. We have Sir Arthur back. It was quite an ordeal but with the help of all concerned he will spend the rest of his time as he wishes."

"How are you feeling?"

"I am doing fine."

"When will you return?"

"I have quite a few items to cover here. I have Greta here to work on the lines. Will know a lot more when I am in London tomorrow. Let me say hello to everyone."

Sir Arthur was brought to the Royal Victoria hospital known as the "Royal". He was there for one day, and Michael had the plane come to Belfast and they flew into London City airport. He accompanied Sir Arthur home where his physician met him. Michael was literally wiped out. The events of the last two weeks were taxing all his faculties and body.

CHAPTER

THIRTY-TWO

AN INTERESTING INTELLIGENCE report came across Michael's desk.

It listed all the military equipment and troops the countries of the Middle East and others sent to the conflict. It did not include Egypt and Syria, the major combatants.

Arab countries sent up to 100,000 troops to Egypt and Syria's front lines. Twenty thousand were sent to Jordan.

The Arab countries were Egypt, Syria, Jordan, Iraq, and several other Arab States were involved in this war providing additional weapons and financing.

Nearly all Arab reinforcements came with no logical plan or support, expecting their hosts to supply them, and in several cases causing logistical problems. On the Syrian front a lack of coordination between Arab forces led to several instances of friendly fire.

Algeria sent 2 squadrons of MIGs to Egypt, also 150 tanks.

The East German Communist Party sent 75 000 grenades, 62 tanks, 12 fighter jets, and 30,000 mines to Syria.

North Korea sent 2 MIGs

Pakistan—their pilots flew combat missions in Syrian aircraft.

Libya—two squadrons of MIGs, and an armored brigade. They also sent financial aid.

Saudi Arabia—20,000 troops in Jordan, 3,000 in Syria and an armored battalion.

Kuwait—3,000 troops to Syria and Egypt.

Morocco—one infantry battalion to Egypt.

Tunisia—2,000 troops to Egypt.

Lebanon enabled Palestine artillery units to operate in their territory. They did not directly take part in the war.

Sudan—3,500-infantry brigade to Egypt.

CHAPTER
THIRTY-THREE

MICHAEL SLEPT IN for one of the few times in his life. He made his way to the office and was greeted enthusiastically. It was now common knowledge of Sir Arthur's rescue and Michael's involvement.

Everyone was excited.

The London Times had a front-page article and picture of Sir Arthur. The press was at Fantastique's door demanding an interview from Michael.

There was never a formal announcement of Michael's position or ownership. There were many articles that were related to the kidnapping. The legal and financial people spread the word. Michael wanted Sir Arthur to make the announcement.

All of these issues were on Michael's mind or agenda. He listed them in his head.

\# 1 Doria

\# 2 Sir Arthur

\# 3 The war

\# 4 The business

The only one he could address at the moment was the business. Greta was here with the new program consisting of sketches and prototypes. Greta had arranged everything. It was laid out in the product center. Many of the prototype garments could be worn by the models employed by Fantastique. It resembled a fashion show.

She had done an outstanding job finalizing and tweaking the collection. She had that touch; Michael knew it the first time he saw her collections for Kaufhaus. They would need three to four days to put everything to bed. There were always changes; the advantage they had was the in-house sample facility. They could see a correction or a new idea in hours.

They broke for lunch.

Michael called Sir Arthur.

"I just want to make sure you're not gallivanting around."

"You can be sure of that. I'm feeling better and in good hands."

Sir Arthur wanted to talk.

"Michael, how are you getting along with my people, are they cooperative?"

"That's the least of your worries; they could not be more willing."

Greta, Michael, and the group of product staff spent the next two days finalizing the collection.

Greta outlined the program to Michael, "we should be able to finish up sometime tomorrow. Your part is actually done. It's the follow up for all of us that needs to be put to bed. Are you free for dinner?"

"Greta, if you are interested in staying in the hotel I would love the time with you, I just can't handle going out and being hounded by the press."

"That's fine. Let's have dinner at 7:00."

At the same time in Germany events occurred, Heinz Adler had been humiliated by Greta. He knew she despised him when they were working together at Kaufhaus. Although he was president of the company he actually answered to Greta. He blamed her for his father's death at the hands of the Israelis. He and his dad were committed Nazis who believed in a Fourth Reich. They had made plans to rebuild the V2 rocket program and relaunch from Egypt to Tel Aviv.

He had made an attempt to kill her when she returned to Dusseldorf to put her affairs in order. He now was the president and CEO of Kaufhaus and not only wanted to avenge his father's death but to show the Aryan National Party that he had a powerful position. He wanted to be a force within the organization. When Heinz spoke to his buyers, they told him how they met Greta in London. They gave him her information in both locations.

He wanted revenge on all counts. Heinz relayed the information on Greta's whereabouts at the meeting of the Aryan Party. There were members who were friends with Herr Adler, Herr Schneider, and Herr Gruder along with his associates who were victims of the Mossad.

It became the major topic on the agenda. The committees decided action should not be taken against Greta Hirsch at this time. She had made fools of their members pumping them for information at their functions. As much as they wanted to eliminate her, they did not want another disaster for the organization. They did not want to mount operations in the U.K. or the United States. It was too dangerous. They were more than willing to rethink the situation if she came to Germany.

Heinz was infuriated with the decision. There was a heated discussion and he walked out of the council meeting. He was going to avenge his father's death and kill Greta Hirsch without their help at any cost. Heinz acted quickly. He had one of his buyers who met Greta call her and obtained her schedule in London.

He then used his contacts to hire two former Waffen SS Troops to assassinate Greta. Heinz was debating with himself whether he would be part of the plan. He made the decision to go to London.

Kurt Lichter and Carl Meiser flew to London and were told where to stay. Both men were well versed in English as well as killing. Kurt new London quite well; he had worked there for over a year quite some time ago. There wasn't a definitive plan, for they did not know if she would be in London at that time. They needed to do some reconnaissance work in order to find out her actual schedule and the best time for an attack. Both men stayed at a two-star hotel near the Connaught. They did not have any exact time for her departure from London.

Aaron and Joshua came to London to see Sir Arthur and Michael. They wanted to thank them for their work to acquire the aircraft and munitions. They played an important role in Israel's ability to strike back after their initial setbacks during the conflict. They both learned from their man in Baghdad of Michael's ordeal. The decision was not to discuss the situation any further. They found Michael in his office.

"We are pleased that Bengy was able to help out. Both of us were rather busy trying to win a war."

"I know you were rather busy."

"I haven't had the time to read all these reports sitting here. I did get the message that we were on the ropes for a while. I guess you guys have to figure out what went wrong. We can't live on the edge."

"Michael, it's complicated. A lot more complex than what happened in the Six Day War. We had to deal with outside sources who tried to dictate the terms and the outcome. But you are right; we took our eye off the ball as you say on your side of the pond."

Michael smiled.

"We should have dinner if you guys are in town tonight."

"That will be great. How's Doria?"

"Great, Greta will join us. She doesn't know you're here."

"Has she recovered from her encounter in Dusseldorf?"

"I don't think so, but she is a realist and a tough lady who will be ready if a similar situation occurs."

The Nazis went about tracking Greta's movements. They were easy to follow. She went from the hotel to the office and back again. She was driven back and forth by company security. The Nazis noticed that she was always aware of any persons near her. Kurt and Carl realized there were few opportunities and places to attempt a kill. Kurt was trying to come up with a plan.

"We have to create a diversion or find a location where she is vulnerable."

Michael organized a private dining room in the hotel. Greta was surprised to see Aaron and Joshua. They had all lived through the V2 rocket affair and now each faced their own demons on different issues. They were all related in one form or another in a bond that never would be broken. There was the usual small talk some retelling their adventures. It seemed the future was uncertain for all.

Greta had an additional day to finalize the line development. Michael wanted to spend at least additional days with Sir Arthur. He was not going home until Arthur was functioning within the parameters set up by his physician. Aaron and Joshua did not have anything specific to discuss with Michael. They had been filled in by Bengy on the events. They did not discuss the arms deal in front of Greta. Sir Arthur was the topic of conversation and the reason why they were here.

The Neo-Nazi's had two options.

\# 1 They would attack when she exited the hotel. They would be lingering either in the lobby or at the door waiting for her to be picked up by Michael's limo or waiting for a taxi.

\# 2 They would attack when she was on route to the office on the roadway. It was a about a fifteen-to-twenty-minute drive to the Fantastique facility.

Option \# 2 seemed to be the better choice. It would give them a better means to control the situation and offer a chance to escape.

They found the location where they would attack. They had a rented car. One would drive while the other would use a machine pistol to strafe the car and kill the occupants. It would give them a better means to control the situation and offer a chance to escape.

The plan had to be revisited for Heinz Adler decided he wanted to be part of the attack.

When the council heard of Heinz's decision, they decided to bless his plan. They needed Heinz for he was now owner of ADM, a maker of engineering and precision tools and machine parts, which had the ability to recreate the V2 rockets.

The foursome said their goodbyes in the lobby. Greta and Michael were both staying on the same floor. Michael suggested they have breakfast together and take the car to the office.

Once in his room he placed a call to Doria and then Abe and Sarah. He caught up on all the news, opened his briefcase and started reading all the intelligence reports he had received from Bengy and the Mossad. There was a mountain of information which he could not possibly absorb in one sitting. He finally set it aside and shut the light.

Greta went over her notes while in bed; she was pleased because Michael was elated with the line. She felt a sense of accomplishment and the start of a new life.

The Neo Nazis wanted to engage Michael's car at a point where it is necessary to be traveling in an area with little traffic. It was critical to start the attack when the auto was traveling less than thirty miles per hour.

Fantastique's complex was located in the vicinity of Covent Garden. It was in the heart of the young fashion and shopping area.

Kurt conducted the operation even though Heinz was present. They looked at the map of the area and went over their usual route to the office. He marked the location where they would attack. Heinz looked it over and agreed. At that time in the morning, the retail stores were closed and almost no tourists. They were not pleased with Heinz's presence but could do little as about it.

Michael's limo was waiting for them and the driver came around and opened the door. It was a different person that had taken them since they arrived.

Michael asked the driver.

"You are new, what happened to our regular man?"

"He is sick today and I am substituting for him."

"You don't mind me asking. We've had some issues lately."

"I don't mind at all. You won't have any problem with me, sir."

The Nazis followed at a safe distance to see if they were going to Fantastique. When they saw them taking the same route, they went ahead to the location where they would attack. They were roughly three to five minutes ahead of Michael's car waiting for their arrival.

The road bent to the left and there was a round-about which forced you to slow down, Fantastique was about 3/4 mile away when the Nazi car came out of a covered area and approached their vehicle.

Heinz was excited. He did not expect to find Michael with Greta and was pleased that he made the decision to kill the traitor and the Jew. Kurt and Heinz opened fire as Michael's car had not picked up speed. When Michael saw the Nazi car pull out to get close to them, he pulled out his Glock and pushed Greta down on the floor. The Nazis' first shots were way off their mark but that would change quickly.

Suddenly two vehicles emerged from two different points which were the roads leading to the round-abouts, firing at the Nazis. Michael's driver pulled over to the side of the road. He reached under the seat and pulled out a machine pistol and started firing. The Nazis realized they were outgunned and tried to flee.

The hail of bullets set the Nazi car on fire and the occupants tried to flee. They were caught in the cross fire and cut down from three directions. The guns were from MI5, the Mossad, and the German police.

Michael had fired three shots and Greta was huddled on the floor. Aaron and Joshua came running over to the car as well as the agents from MI5. Michael got out of the car and ran toward the boys.

"I should punch you guys in the mouth for putting us through this ordeal. What the hell did you know and when?"

"Michael, take it easy. We had to catch them in the act otherwise we couldn't arrest them. If you remember, we had a mole in the Aryan Party and he gave us and the German police all the information.

"We had people watching them before their arrival in the U.K. We came specifically to make sure everything went according to the plan. We are sorry we had to put you through this, but we didn't have much choice."

"I still ought to punch you in the mouth."

They all laughed and hugged one another.

"We have totally eliminated the Aryan Party Organization. The German police and Secret Service have been working with us for the last 6 months to make this happen. Greta's list of the hierarchy made it possible. They are all destined for years behind bars."

Greta started to cry and Michael hugged her.

"It's okay. This should be the end. We survived the bastards; they are dead and we are here to fulfill our dreams. It's a new day."

"If you ever do it again, I will…"

Michael, we know what you will do."

"I can't waste my time talking to you. Greta and I are on our way."

Aaron took Michael by the arm.

"Just one more thing. While you were firing those lousy three shots, we got a call on the radio. You are a proud daddy of a seven-pound boy and Doria is fine."

Michael started crying.

"A boy. He will be named David Jannsen after my dad. The dad I never knew will live again through my son."

He ran to find a phone to call Doria.

THE END

AUTHOR'S NOTES

I thought it would be interesting and informative to review the events after the end of the 1973 Yom Kippur War.

I believe most of us do not realize how the events played out on the world stage. I have tried to give you the bullet points of the events.

These are the key points.

The actual disengagement took place on October 28, 1973 between the Israeli and Egyptian generals.

Kissinger took the proposal to Sadat who agreed.

United Nation check points were brought in to replace Israeli ones; now military supplies were allowed to pass. Prisoners of war were exchanged.

A summit conference in Geneva on December 1973 followed.

The parties of the war—Israel, Syria, Egypt, and Jordan were invited by both the U.S. and the Soviet Union to finalize peace.

The U.N. Security Council passed Resolution 344 which was based on Resolution 388 calling for "a just durable peace".

The conference was forced to adjourn when Syria refused to attend.

Kissinger started Shuttle Diplomacy meeting with Israel and the Arab States.

A peace treaty was signed by Israel and Egypt on January 18, 1974; it was called Sinai I.

Israel agreed to pull back all forces west of the Suez Canal.

On the Syrian front, Shuttle Diplomacy produced a disengagement agreement on May 31, 1974.

These peace discussions were the first time Arab and Israel officials met since the aftermath of the 1948 war.

In response to U.S. support for Israel, the Arab members of OPEC initiated an embargo against the U.S. later joined by others causing an energy crisis in 1973.

In September, 1975 there was a Sinai II; Israel withdrew another 40 km.

The 1978 Camp David Accords were started by Jimmy Carter who invited Sadat and Begin to a summit. They signed a peace treaty in 1979.

The Arab world was outraged at Egypt's peace with Israel. Sadat was deeply unpopular and Egypt was suspended from the Arab League until 1989.

It actually took over six years to sign a peace treaty with Egypt. Until this day, Israel is still at war with Syria.

I have also enclosed a detailed section on the Soviet involvement in the Yom Kippur War. It's a wealth of information that will give you a better understanding what was going on behind the scenes politically and militarily with the superpowers. I felt it was important for the reader to be able to understand the overall significance of the events from an international perspective mainly through the Soviet's point of view and their actions.

The lessons we learned from Soviet behavior and policy in the Arab-Israeli war of 1973 can be divided in to three categories. First, the Soviet involvement demonstrated an impressive ability to follow the rapidly changing situation in the Middle East and to adapt decisions to the course of events on the battlefield. Within less than 24 hours of each of the critical turning points in the crisis, the Soviet leadership appeared to have been aware of the significance of the events, to have reached a decision to act, and then to have actually executed the decision.

For example, shortly after learning that hostilities were imminent, the Soviet leadership, for whatever reason, ordered the evacuation of dependents and advisers from Egypt and Syria and took steps to ensure that information on the Middle East would be available on a priority basis. Once hostilities had begun, within six hours the Soviets had taken a unilateral initiative aimed at achieving a rapid ceasefire that would leave the Arabs with their limited gains without risking defeat. Presumably, the Soviets shared the U.S. and Israeli assessment of the likely outcome of a prolonged war, hoped to help the Syrians preserve their early gains, and were determined to avoid a situation in which they would be called upon to intervene. Although the Syrian position never did completely disintegrate, it was true that a cease-fire on October 7 or 8, for example, would have left the Syrians in control of some of the territory lost in 1967. Even the Egyptian position on the ground at that time was much better than it proved to be on October 22, the day the ceasefire finally was voted in the UN. However, the Egyptians were not ready to stop fighting at such an early date, and the Soviets were not prepared publicly to oppose them. In a variety of ways, however, particularly from October 10 to 12 they were still in the conflict.

The war saw the largest naval confrontation between the United States Navy and Soviet Navy of the entire Cold War. As the United States and Soviet Union supported their respective allies, their fleets in the Mediterranean became increasingly hostile toward each other. The Soviet Operational Squadron had 52 ships in the Mediterranean when the war began, including 11 submarines, some of which carried cruise missiles with nuclear warheads. The United States Sixth Fleet had 48, including two aircraft carriers, a helicopter carrier, and amphibious vessels carrying 2,000 marines.

As the war continued, both sides reinforced their fleets. The Soviet squadron grew to 97 vessels including 23 submarines, while the US Sixth Fleet grew to 60 vessels including 9 submarines, 2 helicopter carriers, and 3 aircraft carriers. Both fleets made preparations for war, and US aircraft conducted reconnaissance over the Soviet fleet. The two fleets began to disengage following the cease fire. During the Kosygin visit to Cairo from October 16 to 19, the Soviets kept pressing for an end of the war. In this aspect of their policy, they came closest to living up to the expectations of détente politics, at least as interpreted and conveyed to them by Kissinger and Nixon. The two architects of détente on the American side did not view the Soviets as delinquent in this aspect of their behavior.

On the Syrian front, the critical period of the war was October 8 to 9, as the Israelis pushed the Syrian forces back to the 1967 cease-fire lines and beyond, and began strategic bombing deep within Syria. The Soviets clearly hoped to prevent further Syrian losses, and, as part of a policy of helping Syria, the Soviets launched an airlift of military equipment on October 10 and encouraged Iraq to join the battle. This aid may have helped somewhat to stabilize the Syrian front by October 13 to 14, by which time the focus of the war was shifting to the Egyptian front.

In Sinai, the critical moment of the war came on October 14, when the Egyptians suffered a major defeat. The night of October 15, the Israeli forces crossed to the west bank of the Suez Canal. On the basis of the first item alone, the Soviets must have foreseen the danger to the Egyptian position, for within 36 hours, Kosygin was on his way to Cairo to urge Sadat to accept an end to the fighting. As the size of the Israeli force on the West Bank grew, Kosygin's appeal for a ceasefire must have gained greater and greater weight with Sadat, who seemed very slow in drawing the appropriate conclusions from the military developments of October 14 and 15.

A second lesson of the war is that the Soviets had a well-developed and responsive airlift and sealift capability. Perhaps some contingency planning had been done for speedy deliveries of military equipment to the Middle East from the moment that hostilities seemed imminent on October 3. Some equipment must have been prepositioned for rapid delivery prior to that date. In any event, the airlift was clearly managed in response to both political and military considerations. Syria, where the needs were initially greatest, received the first infusions of aid. The airlift to Egypt was considerably larger, and may have been partly used as a form of inducement to get Sadat's agreement to a ceasefire. At one point, Iraqi participation seemed important to help stabilize the Syrian front, and on October 14 Iraq received more supplies by air than any other country. Within overall constraints set by logistics, the pattern of resupply seems to reflect a mixture of military and political considerations.

The third aspect of Soviet behavior in the October crisis is that Moscow treated President Sadat as the key person on the Arab side after the first few days. Soviet-Syrian relations had certainly been better than those between Moscow and Cairo, and there is evidence that the Soviets geared their initial policy to Syrian needs, and yet it was Egypt, the more powerful country, that ultimately received most Soviet attention. In particular, the Soviets dealt almost exclusively with Sadat on the ceasefire issue after the war had begun, to the point where President Asad claimed that he had not ever been informed prior to the UN call for a ceasefire on October 22.

The Syrians were preparing for a major counter-attack on October 23, which the Soviets reportedly went to some lengths to prevent once the ceasefire had been voted in the Security Council. Finally, Soviet behavior in the October war suggests a sensitivity to shifts in the balance of forces as a major factor in making decisions.

The Soviet policy was bounded by several general principles, and, within that framework, it was primarily events on the ground that determined specific decisions. The general principles that can most readily be discerned were a desire to retain credibility as a superpower patron with both Egypt and Syria; a determination to avoid full-scale confrontation with the United States; and probably a generalized wish to profit in non-Middle Eastern arenas from the conflict between Israel and the Arabs. Each of these guidelines pulled Soviet leaders in somewhat different directions. Some doctrines indicated caution and restraint.

The Soviets, of course, did not act in the crisis according to textbook rules of détente politics as understood by many Americans. On occasion, Soviet propaganda was inflammatory; the delivery of military equipment may have prolonged the fighting, the threat of unilateral intervention at the close of the war brought the superpowers to a point of near confrontation. And yet, the Soviets, for whatever motives, clearly did try to work for an earlier ceasefire than the Arabs were prepared to accept; and they were prepared to endorse a UN Resolution that called, for the first time, for negotiations between the parties to the conflict.

This mixed record suggests that the Soviets, in an acute crisis such as that of October 1973, were likely to see force and diplomacy as complementary rather than as opposing courses of action. In their view, it is not inconsistent to follow a policy of favoring a "political settlement", while at the same time delivering the means to launch a war nor is it inconsistent to work for a ceasefire while mounting an airlift and sealift of military equipment to clients engaged in actual hostilities. What the Soviets were not prepared to do was to see their relations with Egypt and Syria destroyed by their unwillingness to help the Arabs recover their territory in a war that the Soviets had repeatedly termed as justified. In large measure, this had to do with the position of the Soviet Union as a superpower. Its prestige was clearly on the line. At the same time, the Soviets were not anxious to become directly involved in the fighting, with all the dangers of confrontation that this held. To this end, they remained in close contact with the United States throughout the war, and, from the perspective of the White

House, they seemed generally cooperative in efforts to achieve a ceasefire in place.

The basic rule governing Soviet policymaking in an acute crisis was to use enough force to retain credibility with one's friends and clients and to engage in enough diplomacy to ensure that the crisis does not lead to superpower confrontation. The proper balance of these two key ingredients determined the behavior of the United States, internal Soviet politics, and, very importantly, the actual course of events in the crisis area.

SOURCES

1. The October War—El Gammasy

2. The Arab Israel Conflict—A guide the perplexed—Ian Bickerton

3. Israel intelligence and the 1973 Arab Israeli War—Mathew Penney

4. The Yom Kippur War—The Epic Encounter that Transformed the Middle East—Rabonovich

5. Tears Of Upheaval—Henry Kissinger

6. Conversations between Brent Scowcroft and Henry Kissinger at Washington University

7. USSR in the World Conflict—Soviet arms diplomacy—Bruce Porter

8. Anwar Sadat's Grand Strategy—James Bean and Craig Conrad

9. The Yom Kippur War—The Sinai—Simon Dunston and Kevin Lyles

10. The Peace Process—William Quandt

11. Palestine and the Arab conflict—Chanes Smith

12. Arab-Israeli Air War—Shlomo Aloni

13. The Arab Israeli Wars—Herzog

14. Friendly Enemies Israel and Jordan—David Rodman

15. Inside Israel's Northern Command—The Yom Kippur War on the Syrian Border—Dani Asher

16. Baghdad—City of Peace City of Blood—Justin Marozzi

17. Yasser Arafat—A political biography—Stephen Robert

18. Historical Dictionary of the Northern Ireland Conflict—Cordon Giuseppe

19. Hope against History—Jack Holland

20. Explaining Northern Ireland—John McCarthy and Brendan O'Leary

21. Golda Meir, an outline of a unique life—from the Golda Meir Center for Political Leadership

22. Golda Meir—Encyclopedia of Zionism Israel

23. The Internet and the research done for I Shall Know who I Am and A Cause for All.

24. Golan heights—Peter Adams

25. The story of my life—Moshe Dyan

26. Soviet Strategy in the Middle East—George Breslauer

27. Patterns of Soviet Policy towards the Middle East—Robert Freedman

28. The United States and the Soviet Union in the Middle East—O.M. Smolansky